Personal Best

Jonesy Elise

Content Notes

Personal Best deals with the aftermath of divorce and references miscarriages and their impact on people and relationships. To learn more about miscarriage support, *Through the Heart* is an excellent resource.

This story also contains consensual sex acts. Some of these acts enter BDSM territory, including spanking, slapping, and choking. As much care has been taken to depict a BDSM relationship safely and sweetly, a spicy romantic comedy should not be a substitute for a How-to Guide.

Content also includes an off-page trip to the emergency room and an off-page car accident.

Finally, although not explicitly stated, the main character is going through symptoms of depression. If you or someone you know needs help in managing depression, seek resources through your preferred healthcare provider.

To anyone who ever felt like they didn't belong—especially at a gym.

Chapter One

I had never won anything in my life. So, I treasured the glossy cardstock possessing my pass to one free class at EverGreen & Fit Studios. This was a sign from the Fates. Things were going to look up—for once.

Not much of a gym rat, I arrived wearing one of my cartoon possum T-shirts and my old high school gym shorts. Since hitting my thirties, acquaintances had expressed bizarre excitement over me still fitting into my old shorts. They shouldn't be so thrilled. The elastic was one wash away from giving up altogether, and at the time my mom had filled out the form to purchase said shorts, she thought it was a great idea to order them two sizes too big. Which meant that almost a decade and a half later, I could say I wear the same shorts I wore in high school to the impressed coos of far too many women conditioned into believing the teen *girl* body was the ideal.

The woman at the front desk, who was refreshingly older than me, scooted a clipboard toward me. Her strawberry blonde hair sat on her head like cotton candy. I at first thought she wore a headband, but it was her giant glasses on the top of her head. "Fill these forms out."

"Forms? As in plural?" I asked in disbelief. What beyond *I'm Saoirse. Thirty-seven. Watch out for the right knee* did they need? "You're not going to sell my information, are you?"

Front-desk Fran, my new name for my name tag-less friend, narrowed her eyes. "I don't think so?"

At first, the information was cursory: name, address, phone number. Those identifiers left the EverGreen & Fit pen with little thought. I paused at *Emergency Contact.* It used to be Chris.

Could it still be Chris? Maybe it was one of the things relinquished when I filled out the divorce papers. That left whom?

As I considered my emergency contact options, a gaggle of gym-goers strode through the turnstile with a steady succession of beeps and clicks after they scanned their passes. Fran gave those aged suburban athletes a quick smile or nod.

I hovered the ballpoint pen over the empty box. My mom and sister were an entire mountain range away. Mom wasn't necessarily spry with the mental faculties of an *emergency* contact. Older, wiser, and overall better human being, Fiona would tell me an emergency contact needed to be in the same county, at least. I put Tina, my boss. If I passed out on a stair climber and had to be taxied home under Tina's care, she'd be happy to be there for an employee of such dependability as me. That, and everyone else on my contact list chose Chris over me.

For goals, I considered *achieve the body of Thor* and *world domination.* The real reason, of course, was I hated how I could barely carry a conversation while ascending a flight of stairs. But no more! For I was Super Gym Membership Woman! I wrote *Kegels that reach enlightenment.* The next two blanks were *Current Weight* and *Goal Weight.*

"In the year of our Lord now, do you think people still go to gyms to lose weight? I thought we were past that."

Front-desk Fran's narrow lips hung agape. More beeps and clicks sounded behind me as people shoved their way through the turnstile. This time, they arrived without a gesture of acknowledgement from my clipboard-wielding friend behind the desk.

I put *IDGAF* in both blanks and handed the clipboard back. I claimed to have made peace with the jiggly bits of my body a few years ago. I figured if there was one benefit of being middle-aged in today's society, it was giving less and less of a shit about beauty standards. But life was a journey. Some days my cellulite didn't get to me. Others, I'd cave and buy a snake oil salve, the key to smooth thighs.

"And I need to see your ID," Fran said with a sigh.

"Need a blood sample, too?" I punctuated my question with a snort to show Fran I meant it in jest. However, a half-assed set at an open mic night performed to a brick wall audience had better reactions. I fished my license out of my sock and sunk my face into a clownish apology as a layer of ankle sweat coated it.

Front-Desk Fran cringed as she studied my ID and the info on the clipboard. "The last name on the form is different from the one here."

"It's because I'm a spy. Your keen observation thwarted my plan." I waited for a beat as Front-Desk Fran blinked at me. "A joke. I haven't officially changed my name *back*. Divorced." Eighteen months passed since I filled out those papers on Chris's initiation, but it continued to feel strange to admit it. I had hit the reset button on my life and still was a bit self-conscious about it.

Frannie's (we were getting close now, so I could add syllables of affection to her name) forehead creased. I couldn't tell if her skin was naturally this ruddy or if I was starting to piss her off. She lightly penned *Garfield* over my maiden name *Hooper*.

She asked about my shoe size and bent down to search for it among the cubbies below. I turned around and leaned back against the desk to take in the world of the EverGreen & Fit Studios.

Despite the gym's name, nothing was in the shade of *evergreen*. They chose a green color that looked like the spawn of mint and pea green, and it was everywhere. Walls, doors, signage, the freaking shirt Frannie wore. Occasionally, there would be a beige-y hiccup of color in the green. The air reeked of rubber, sweat, and a hint of lemongrass, the smell of a seance on leg day.

The *thwack!* of the cycling shoes hitting the counter pulled me from my interior design daze.

As I wiggled into the shoes, leaning against the desk, I knocked over a stack of cardstock flyers that had been piled next to the gargantuan hand sanitizer. I scrambled to pick them up and scanned the familiar fonts and glossy sheen. They were postcards advertising *First Class Free.* A sick feeling tightened my throat.

I should've known.

I had won the free class at a Crazy Days event in Gorda Vista, the slice of suburbia I wound up in. It was especially important for work, making sure all the custom labeled awnings, tents, signs, banners for the various businesses who hired us looked good. I had wandered among the aisles of business tents to land some of the swag I helped them print—pens, a lanyard, and something that could only be described as a doohickey.

Maybe it was the shots of schnapps offered by the local distillery that had done it to me, but I filled out my name for a drawing. A few more swiped shots of schnapps later, they announced my name at the end of the festival. And it had felt as if I won the

Olympics, a peace prize, a scientific breakthrough. I, Saoirse Hooper, won.

But I hadn't.

The free class was offered to any schmo, and I was drawn in on some promise that I won this. I shuffled to the cycling studio, where already most of the bikes were taken by people who had matching Spandex sets and ponytails with zero flyaways. They were toned, tanned, and serious—everything not pictured next to the definition of my name.

The last bike available was front and center.

I clipped into the pedals. Oof, at the current bike setting, the seat intruded my crotch, and I pedaled on my tiptoes to complete a rotation. I needed to adjust the bike. How was I going to do that?

A tenor voice boomed over the speakers, "WHO'S READY TO PARTY?!"

The class answered in a chorus of *woo*. I shifted forward to the skinnier part of my seat to see the source of our head party animal.

The perfect symmetrical specimen of masculinity entered the room. Tall but not too tall, fit but not some 'roided-out superhero, a healthy pallor to his skin but not fake or at-risk-of-skin-cancer tanned. He was adorned in a tank top in the EverGreen & Fit brand of green and shorts, compression layered under a loose pair. Honestly, he was the type of attractive I turned my gaze from, as if looking at him was a solar eclipse. The unfortunate thing about his appearance was his hair coiffed to look like a cockatiel.

"For those who are new or who are forgetful, I'm Beau Bishop, and I'm taking you on an adventure today. We're going to warm up for the next five minutes. You can crank that shaft between your legs right for more resistance and left to ease it. If you need to brake, hold that giant red knob down. And don't worry, we'll be going hard and fast in no time for those who like to get a little filthy."

I giggled. Were we talking cycling or fucking? I looked around the room to see if I'd discover some camaraderie in recognizing the double entendre. I got nothing from the cycling elite, holier than thou copy-pasters. Copy-pasters because they were the kinds of people to repeat something only if it fed into the suburban lifestyle.

"Set your resistance between twenty and forty and keep your RPM between eighty and one hundred."

He might as well have told me to press the *pif-flepaff* to get the *farfegnugen* to *jimblejamble*—that was how much sense he was making, but I gave the knob in front of me a twist to the right and started to pedal. When the pop song repeated its chorus—the one with the lyrics I found stupid the first time I had ever heard it—I had entered my version of Purgatory: cardio exercise soundtracked by the cringiest pop songs.

The secretly perverted cycling instructor with the ridiculously alliterative name squeezed his hand over the mic of his headset. "You're Saoirse?"

I nodded. He scored a point for pronouncing my name correctly. Most people who looked like they spend more time wooing and cardio-ing slaughtered my name. *Sours* or *Sah-oy-ers,* never *Sir-sha.*

"You don't have the arm weights. Don't worry, I got you covered." Again, what he said was Greek to me. He disappeared into a green and wood grain colored closet off the cycling room. He returned with a tiny set of two-pound weights and placed them in the basket hooked off the seat of the bike. I clenched my butt cheeks. His hands were awfully close to my ever-flattening derriere.

"Looks like your seat is too high. Step off for a moment."

I stopped pedaling. One of my shoes dislodged from the clip. The other foot was stuck spinning. Ow! The free pedal whacked me right in the calf, leaving a mark.

"Always remember to hit the brake if you're stopping. It's right in front of you." He pointed to the knob.

"Sorry." I uttered an unnecessary apology because my Enneagram two profile said I was apt to apologize for things I was never in control over. Some rounds of therapy told me I did it because I was a millennial woman raised with micro-traumas, if a passive-aggressive Midwestern mom with an unrelenting martyr complex was trauma-inflicting. I thought it was just the default setting of being a femme from a flyover state.

"No worries." He adjusted the seat. His concentrating breaths rumbled over the speakers. He put his hand over the black cushy end of the mic again. "You should be good now. Funny shirt." He smiled. A bit of wisdom crinkled around his puppy-dog brown eyes. He was younger than me but not a baby.

"Thanks. I drew it." I was wearing my shirt of an angry possum, *Social Hiss-tancing*. I drew it back when my thirties were fresh, when I thought the whole working for a printing business was a stopover before my real career of putting my art on ItsyBizzy and selling T-shirts, postcards, and magnets with my designs. But I threw in the towel, as they say, when the art to happiness ratio dwindled. All I had to speak of for this era was a single box of unsold merchandise.

I clipped back in. He was right; the adjustment felt so much better.

I picked up speed on the pedals and adjusted the resistance. The numbers changed on the dashboard in front of me. Okay, I was getting a handle on this.

The music switched to a club rap song that I thought had been cast into the fires of "Things We Regretted in 2007" along with skinny scarves and pageboy hats.

Beau ordered us to crank the resistance and stand up on the pedals. "Keep your hips back, booty over your seat, chest forward, and chin down."

My body contorted to the odd game of Simon Says. I stumbled, catching myself on the handlebars.

"Feel the support from your core," he added.

That correction was for me. He saw me falter and had to point it out. How did one feel support from their core? Brief looks at the copy-pasters in the mirror did not provide any concrete examples of the concept.

Then a Katy Perry song blared over the speakers, the inspirational one that made girl bosses sprout from the ground much like a Cabbage Patch doll. I wasn't in Purgatory. I was in Hell. Thankfully, the resistance and RPM were at a perfectly medium territory. Maybe I could get the hang of this bike in Hell.

The chorus kicked in, the one about bringing out a person's inner arsonist.

Beau shouted into the mic, "You got over the hardest part by being here. Ask yourself—are you going to shine? Are you going to give it your all? I know you will. Push that resistance up by one or two and give me 105 to 120. Show me your fireworks, baby!"

Oh Jesus. He won the genetic lottery in looks, but his command of inspirational prose was enough to make whatever tinge of a clit boner I had shrivel back. But the crowd ate it up! Chirps of "Yeah!" and the ever-so-present "Woo!" accentuated the song's beat. I picked up the pace and reached a peak. The numbers on the dashboard read 95. So, I had to do better.

I pushed and pushed. And huffed and huffed. The strands of my faded burgundy hair from my sloppy ponytail stuck to my sweat. My saliva tasted of iron. I got 101—nowhere near the 105 I needed to be at. Maybe these were vanity numbers. I glimpsed to the right of me. Nope. One among the throng of toned and serious was up to 120.

Beau announced, "Pull it back to an easy jog, eighty to one hundred."

I was at an easy jog? I was sweaty, winded, and about ready to barf up any vital organs, and I was at an *easy* jog? No, I was behind.

And it hit like a dodgeball to the face. Tears pricked my eyes. *My best wasn't good enough. I was behind the real adults.* I laid my arms across the handlebars and buried my face in them. I stopped pedaling. Another matching *thwack* marked my other calf. I'd walk out of here with twin bruises.

"If you need to stop, press your brake," Beau said.

"I know," I murmured into my arms.

Real adults didn't treat a free class won in a schnapps-induced stupor as the golden ticket to their dreams. They scheduled workouts in their matching sets. They had been good to their cardiovascular systems so an easy jog was just that. They probably never got winded going up a flight of stairs. They didn't peak in a career drowned in defeat. And they probably didn't dramatically obsess over workout playlists nor associated a pop song as being the bane of their existence. But me? I was a sweaty emotional mess in an oversized possum T-shirt.

"Keep going. You're worth it." His voice was soft with encouragement, as if I were a baby taking its first step.

The speakers shuffled and crackled. I sensed that Beau had leaped off the bike and put his hand over the microphone. "Are you okay?"

I could be. I didn't know the party I'd be attending was going to be a pity one. It didn't have to be like this. I had two legs and a middle finger. I swung my leg over the seat, stood up, and checked the nose ring in my left nostril. "I'm fine."

I walked out. The door drowned out the music. I kicked off the shoes and placed them on Frannie's front desk and half wedged my feet into my street shoes. I hobbled into the parking lot with my shoes barely clinging to my feet.

I started my car and pulled out of the parking lot. I didn't *just* quit. Fools continued to do something even when it was painful. Wise people—and now I psyched myself up to believe I was a part of the wise—knew when to pack it in.

Or so I told myself.

Chapter Two

Like any working woman, I multi-tasked in the morning: I commuted to work and talked to my sister. The conversations weren't really a two-way, she shares, I share sort of deal. It was usually me going "Yeah," "uh-huh" and then "that's wild" on repeat until my sister was done monologuing about life living near Mom.

"She called me at work to see if I could help program the remote *again*," Fiona said.

"That's wild."

"How's work going for you?"

"Yeah." I stopped in my tracks. She wasn't complaining about Mom for once. "Oh, me. Um, it's alright."

"I recognize that singsong response. It's what a person says before adding *but...*"

I was not blind to the fact that I had the job equivalent of a bologna sandwich—easy and adequate. Tina and I kept on top the moderate number of orders we'd print. Sometimes I'd design something, putting my art degree to good use. Other times—and by other times, I mean most of the time—people ordered designs off templates that I had to lazily upload on a computer. When I was trying to get my ItsyBizzy business of stupid animals saying inane things off the ground, Tina gave me free rein on the equipment as long as I had her business orders fulfilled and paid for the supplies I used.

The *but* my sister perceived was that finances at work weren't ideal, especially as customers flocked to the cheap and worse customer service of online printers. When the shop would have to eventually shutter up like the dinosaur it was, I wasn't necessarily ready to leap to a backup plan. So far, my backup plan was staying in Gorda Vista, my ex-husband's hometown. "I was so busy with banners last weekend." Not a lie and not giving my sister the ammunition to fire off a *Move back home.*

"How are your friends?"

That bitch. She knew when I followed Chris across the country that I spent all my relationship currency on him and not friendships. Not the brightest life choice, especially after a divorce, but I couldn't stress enough how amazing most evenings were when all I had to do was heat up dinner, read a book, and go to bed at a decent hour. I brought up the name of one of my favorite authors. "Rachel always has a good story to tell over a glass of rosé."

"You've never mentioned Rachel before," Fiona replied.

Yeah, because when you call, I listen to how Mom fell for a scam email.

I tossed out a casual, "And I'm due for some mimosas with Clarissa." Clarissa was my hairstylist who I hadn't seen for a while. And boy, were my roots coming in *silver*.

"Just know we're always here for you, Sir."

Right, so I could move back to the Midwest and remind myself why following a man back to his hometown was the better idea. I could see it now. I would arrive at one family event five minutes before Fiona's designated "start time" and my dutiful sister or Mom would mention something about how *long* they had been waiting for me. I'd run out that door back to my empire of mediocrity out West, leaving streams of smoke behind me like a cartoon roadrunner. "Yeah, I know," I answered.

Later that day, I kicked open the back door of The Mighty Pen Printers. I had finished a batch of T-shirts for a bowling league team, and the place stunk of fresh plastisol ink. With the backdoor propped, I whipped off my face mask.

My phone vibrated in the front pocket of my apron. I wasn't a popular contact, so I figured I'd block the spam I was inevitably receiving. But the number was a local number. *For EverGreen & Fit Studios.* What the hell did they want? I answered. "Hi, this is Sir."

"Am I speaking to Saoirse Garfield?" a familiar man's voice asked.

Familiar yet loaded with the smarmy cheerfulness that was about to sell me some shit. "May I ask who's calling?"

"This is Beau Bishop from EverGreen & Fit Studios. I wanted to check that you were okay after leaving my class early."

"Uhh." The *uh* was completely loaded. I was unprepared for a follow-up to my dramatic exit from the green and fit world. "Yeah, I'm okay." A small facsimile of a clench in my throat from class returned. I wasn't about to divulge to a silly dude with even goofier hair and a ridiculously alliterative name the whirlpool of negative self–talk I circled in during a damn Katy Perry song.

"I'm trying to gauge where we could improve to meet your needs. To improve the fitness experience."

I picked at the crackled dead possum cartoon I had printed on the apron ages ago. "I'm kind of a curmudgeon–y weirdo. I think a gym appealing to my demographic would go belly up."

"We want to be a place where all sorts of people feel welcome."

Bull and shit. "I appreciate the call. I'm sure you could sell sand to the desert, but I'm not interested." As I turned the phone so I could press the red button to end the call, a flurry of *No's* rushed from the tiny speaker. He was sort of adorable in his relentlessness. I returned the phone to my ear. "You really want to hear what I think?"

"Bring it on."

I sat on a ream of neon orange paper and sighed. "For starters, I felt deceived. I supposedly won a free class from a drawing, but it turns out to be a deal you offer to all new customers. I wanted to be special, and it felt a little assy when I wasn't."

"I'm sorry we made you feel that way. I'm certain if I was in your shoes, I'd feel the same. Let me make it up to you."

I could sense a green water bottle with the Ever-Green & Fit logo in my near future. It would belong on my mantel next to pens, a lanyard, and my new little doohickey. "Do I have to step into that green monstrosity of a gym?"

"Would you like to meet in a more neutral territory?"

"That's an option?" The phone call was only going to more and more unexpected places.

"Tell you what, right off the gym's parking lot is part of the Red Sequoia Trail. We can have a walk and a quality assurance meeting. When are you free?"

Automatically, I replied, "After work. 5:15."

"See you then."

What the ever-loving fuck did this Beau Bishop get me to agree to?

Chapter Three

I hoped this meeting wasn't going to sneak in some outdoorsy bootcamp moves. I needed high knee lifts and burpees like I needed a hole in the head. I ensured that our meeting would be strictly talk, wearing my clunky Doc Marten boots, distressed jeans, and my couch potato sweatshirt—my drawing of a basic russet potato rotting on a loveseat.

At the trail gate, he waited for me, dressed in a matching green tracksuit. His hair was still shaped like a cockatiel's.

"I really appreciate you meeting with me, Saoirse."

"Call me Sir."

He opened the gate to the trail and turned his head quizzically. "Like a knight?"

"Or your dungeon master. Fits me better than Saoirse."

"Another funny shirt, I see. Did you draw that one as well?"

He had listened to me? "Yup."

"You're an artist, then."

"Ha, no. I work for the printing company downtown, The Mighty Pen. This isn't art. More like the scribblings of a mad woman." Discussing my failed ItsyBizzy store in the shadow of my failed cycling class sort of put a sour taste in my mouth. "Let's cut to the chase and discuss some quass."

He flickered another look of confusion at me.

"A portmanteau of quality assurance. *Quass*."

"Do other people say that?"

"I dunno. We could make it a thing."

"So, the winner's drawing was misleading. Our commitment to the color green is"—he looked down at his dark green matching zip-up and track pants set—"a bit much. What else?"

"The whole *woo* of it all. Even on the rare occasions where I liked doing some cardio, I never

ever wanted to yell *woo* or any variations thereof. It feels *forced*."

"Interesting."

"And the music! The music! You were a 'Mambo No. 5' away from releasing an old god from the Earth's core and cursing us all to a thousand years of the 'Macarena.'"

"Duly noted. Anything else?"

"You. Is Beau Bishop even your real name? It's so literal. 'Hi, my name means handsome, and I am handsome. Thanks for noticing.'"

"Beau Bishop is my name. Need to see my birth certificate?" His mouth curled into a smirk. "You think I'm handsome?"

"Everyone thinks you're handsome. You're the type of good-looking who makes a normie like me have to dig for flaws. Like, I kind of hope you're mean or stupid just to balance the aesthetic out. Except you're not mean. I've leveled about fifty different criticisms at you, and you're not defensive. You're listening to me. And I haven't felt listened to..." I shuddered at the thought.

He gestured for us to turn around and head back to the parking lot. Our walk down a stretch of suburban trail was coming to an end. Strangely, I dragged my feet a little to ward off the outcome.

"I should make it up to you," he said.

He'd probably offer me a grab bag of green merch. Useless crap, the tokens of forgiveness every business had. "Do I get a green koozie?"

"How about a free one-on-one?"

"As in you, me..." My face heated up at the idea, as if I was a thirteen-year-old with a crush.

"And the bikes between our legs." His eyes sparkled a bit. He knew he said something a bit *saucy.*

"You don't have to." The Midwestern nice leaped out of me. I had practiced so much humility and disguising any sort of wants with it, that side of me tumbled out involuntarily.

"I want to, Sir."

When he said it like that... "This time tomorrow?"

"Perfect."

Tomorrow was Friday. Technically, I had a Friday night date.

Chapter Four

O ver my lunch break, I bought some bicycle shorts with a matching sports bra from the running store down the street. No more gym shorts that were old enough to vote. But planning to go straight from work to the gym, I realized I hadn't packed a T-shirt and wasn't comfortable enough in my gym journey to let myself hang out in bike shorts and a bra. I threw on the shop's test T-shirt with every plastisol ink design from the past five years. It resembled a Jackson Pollock painting of tee ball leagues, bachelorette parties, and charity 5K-runs.

I arrived at the gym earlier than our agreed upon time. He was already waiting in his layered shorts and now green long-sleeved T-shirt. He had the biggest grin on his face and was practically shaking. "I was at the store today to get some toothpaste, and I found something for you that might really change your experience here."

He handed me a pair of cheap, red-tinted sunglasses. Red and green were opposites on the color wheel. The red neutralized the green into brown. I put them on. "Ah yes. Much better."

I followed him through the gym, past the weight room, and down the hall to the studios for class. "Your goals... just improving your fitness levels?" Beau called back to me.

"Sure. I'd love to go up a flight of stairs without losing my breath."

He leaned against a door labeled *Studio 2*. "Do you know your body fat composition?"

I wasn't sure if I should be offended by the question. I rolled my shoulders back and put my hands on my hips, ready to argue about beauty standards and everything wrong with fitness culture. "Do you?"

"Yeah, about thirteen percent." He said it as if he was commenting on the color of the sky. *Why yes, the sky is blue. Hi, I'm Beau. Yes, I am thirteen percent fat. Salads possess more fat than I have.*

I quirked a speculative brow in his direction. "Is this the moment where you try to sell me a bunch of supplements and powders?"

"Do you want supplements and powders?"

"No."

"Then eat whatever the fuck you want." He donkey-kicked the door behind him open.

The sudden dirty mouth of his betrayed the cheerleader persona I had built around him. Or around any workout instructor. Had I found the hallowed safe place where I could say all the fucks I didn't give?

Because the cycle studio had a class in session, we met in "the hot yoga room." Thankfully, it was also at a normal room temperature and humidity levels, a few fitness tidbits I'd learned from Beau in the last five minutes.

He had carted in a couple of bikes into the room. Soon he showed me the billion ways the bike could be adjusted. With a few twists, slides, and adjustments, the bike fit my height and legs perfectly. Almost. Beau scowled a lot at the machine, making persnickety centimeter by centimeter adjustments.

I began pedaling and playing around with the numbers. At twenty resistance, I easily reached ninety RPMs, which, thanks to my enthusiastic instructor, I learned meant revolutions per minute. He told me to crank the resistance to forty-five and climb. I stood on the pedals and pumped.

"Reach your hips farther back." He jumped on the bike next to me and hovered his butt over the seat. "Like this."

Not gonna lie, I kind of enjoyed being instructed to look at his ass. Cycling did his body good.

"But keep your back flat—aim to have your sternum burst right through your chest."

"Okay, it's this shit—that instruction makes zero sense. No one can manipulate their sternum."

He hopped off the bike. "Can I touch you?"

"Sure. Fine. Whatever." Three words of mine that actually meant *holy shit, yes.*

With a graze of his fingers, he touched me on either side of my hips. He gently tugged them back, moving my butt closer to him. I shifted my grip.

"Don't move your hands!"

Can you still say *yes, daddy* when a man is younger than you? I adjusted my hold on the handlebars.

"Feel that stretch in your hamstrings?"

And that nervous tingle in my panties? "Yup."

His fingers tapped a spot in the middle of my back. My shoulders automatically rolled back, moving my chest forward. "Good," he said. "Now climb. Give me an RPM of sixty-five."

I picked up pace.

"Don't shift your hips from side to side. Keep yourself steady. Yes, like that."

If I went through enough of this kind of training, I might develop a praise kink.

His gaze met mine in the gym mirror. "If you feel safe and steady, close your eyes."

How could I not follow that order? I squeezed my eyes shut. My body vibrated as I sensed him watching me. "Feel how the power is coming from your glutes and not just your quads? This will give you more power for climbs."

"I think so?" I popped one eye open.

"Getting the hang of it?"

I nodded.

"Unclip and step off."

He nudged me out of the way and adjusted the handlebars and seat to the opposite of what he had carefully set them to. "Remember how the bike felt in a jog and climb. Adjust it to fit."

I lowered the seat and slid it forward. I clipped in and stood up, getting a feel for where to adjust the handlebars. "Does this look good?"

His puppy-dog gaze moved over me, and his mouth curled into a tiny smirk. "Move the handle-bars up a scooch."

I scooched as I was told. I arched an eyebrow to invite a bit more of those positive affirmations.

"Now we can take this up a notch." A remote appeared in his hand. He pressed it, and Backstreet Boys blasted over the speakers.

When this song came out in middle school, I hat-ed it because I was a contrarian little shit. Hearing it now gave those nostalgic, warm fuzzies. When the key change hit, the music compelled me to sing.

"It's good to sing while riding. It ensures you're breathing properly!" He joined in, his ski-slope hair flopped with every exaggerated move of his lips.

We sweat and bad karaoked our way through the greatest hits of my middle and high school years. Studying myself in the room-sized mirror, I prob-ably needed to invest in some waterproof mascara because at the end of the session, I was a shiny, sloppy mess with black smudges around my blue eyes. Good thing someone gave me some red sun-glasses to step out of the studio in.

As I changed my shoes and toweled the sweat off my face, he asked, "A better free class than last time?" He sprayed the bikes down and wiped the sweat off them. I had left an embarrassing wet spot on the seat.

"That was..." *Don't say something cheesy, don't say something cheesy.* "Exhilarating!" What did I say about *not* being cheesy?

"Would you be interested in seeing each other again?"

My body felt like the snowy channels on old-school televisions, fizzy and sparkling. Was this a date? I croaked out an "I would" and rubbed my lips together. When Chris and I were dating, he had told me he loved my sensuous lips. I was going to use them to my advantage. I cleared my throat. "There's this cocktail place I'd like to try. We could—"

He blinked rapidly. "I meant for personal training. My rate is seventy-five dollars an hour."

Like the moron I was, I thought he meant a date. "I was joking, of course. No, I'd be totally into some more personal training." How could I stick the landing of this terrible, terrible dismount? "Seventy-five you say? What do you recommend? Five or six days a week? I was leaning more toward six, so—"

"Five sessions a week is plenty."

"Great. See you..." I searched his gaze for the answer.

In unison, we said, "Monday."

Blowing a healthy chunk of change on some personal training sessions under the duress of a lady boner wasn't exactly the smartest move. I wasn't Ms. Moneybags, necessarily. I did, however, have a healthy sum of money after Chris and his new wife bought me out of my portion of what was once our home. And since I wasn't the one who demolished a marriage under the pretense of falling in love with someone else, Chris offered me a healthy alimony to ameliorate the gaping wound in me caused by the betrayal. I guess burning through my ex-husband's money was what society expected out of me, the scorned and crafty divorced woman.

Beau ran my credit card; the sessions were now prepaid. We were beginning our beautiful transactional relationship.

Chapter Five

Confession time: I practically burnt my clit off with how much I used my vibrator this weekend. Ole Reliable, my pet name for the space age looking phallus with the weird, rubbery nubs near its base, had been collecting dust. If I drew a graph of my horniness in relation to how sexy I felt, it'd be two straight lines scraping the bottom of the grid. So, if habit determined behavior, I was practically a nun. And I was pretty sure nuns had masturbated more than I had in the last few years.

But my libido returned with a vengeance. I usually tried to keep the visitors of my reveries fictional—pansexual vampires or a wholesome seven-foot blue alien with a monster dick. If I needed something more human to get me there, I focused on a character from a TV show I found hot. The point is, the tremors Ole Reliable gave me were not to be associated with anything in the non-fiction realm because I had some prurient view of consent. And having to make eye contact with the current object of my fantasies put me in a guilt tailspin.

In fairness, I was dragging Ole Reliable across my nipples, thinking about some green alien with a Scottish accent demanding I initiate him in the ways of human procreation. For the sake of the fantasy, I imagined myself to be in some kind of dirndl that had been expertly untied. I massaged my inner thigh with the vibrating, silicone dick because green Scottish aliens liked to build the tension. And then right as I headed for the sweet spot, my dirndl became an oversized T-shirt saturated in plastisol ink; the green-skinned alien became a certain instructor with boy band hair. The memory of Beau's fingers, barely moving my hips or pressing on the middle of my back sent me over the edge again and again.

At this point, in both my fictional and non-fictional relationships, I'd attempt to leave some mystery—cool off contact, make other plans.

But. I. Prepaid.

So after a weekend of way too much objectification, I dragged myself to the gym, darting my gaze anywhere but the direction of Beau Bishop. Thank goodness for red-tinted sunglasses.

Monday's session was a change in pace. Beau showed me around the weight room. If my first time cycling drove me to quit and bolt, it didn't take much imagination to realize when it came to weight lifting, I was about as fearful as a cat with a vacuum cleaner. I'd claw myself onto any solid mass of safety, which happened to be Beau, encouraging me to commit to a leg day with free weights. And as if I had predicted today's feeling, I wore another original T-shirt design, a high-strung calico cat, clinging to a coffee cup for dear life. I had drawn in squiggly letters, *What do you mean coffee gives me anxiety?*

"Weight lifting? Won't that make me look like the Hulk? Lou Ferrigno, not Mark Ruffalo."

"No. You won't be lifting heavy enough *and* if the next words out of your mouth are 'I want the long and lean look,' I'm going to tell you, there's no such thing as lengthening your muscles. They're attached to your bones. If you want to look lean, you'll have to work that out in the kitchen."

"The kitchen?"

"High–protein, low–fat diet."

"Oh."

"Strength training is an excellent way to improve balance and prevent osteoporosis."

"I'm old but not that old."

"When it comes to health, most of the time, you can never be too early." He sat on the ground and patted the workout mat. I took that as my cue to sit next to him. He showed me weight-free hip thrusts to "help activate my glutes."

As I shoved my pelvis into the air, filthy thoughts of me straddling Beau as he demonstrated a hip thrust entered my mind. In fairness, *I'd* be the added weight helping him strengthen. Yet I wasn't sure what was more erotic: sitting on Beau's crotch as he hip thrusted or watching Beau as he studied my ass to make sure I was giving that final squeeze at the top of my thrust?

He stood over me and asked, "What did you do this weekend?"

"This." I gestured toward my hips humping the air. "Over and over again from Friday to Sunday," I joked in a bizarre truth–adjacent way.

"So, you stayed in then?"

"And got groceries, cleaned, bought more workout clothes, read a book."

He motioned for me to move onto my side. I bent my legs at a perfect ninety degrees. "Put light pressure on your outside knee with your hand and lift your knee against that pressure, keeping your ankles together."

Clamshells. The move discovered a muscle in my ass I thought never existed and, to reiterate, was strangely sexual to me. With the way Beau's gaze followed me, the blood flow that I had diverted to my pelvis all weekend was not going to go to my brain. I was on the verge of a self-inflicted lobotomy.

"What book are you reading?" The Mormon-like genuine interest he expressed was as sadly adorable as an ASPCA ad.

My tongue was flexing to say something Oprah recommended but with activating my glutes, I embraced honesty. "*Mating with the Man from Mars.*"

The reach of his eyebrows said it all. *Sir, you're a sad, perverted woman.*

"It's a meditation on what it means to be human," I added.

And I identified my problem. Beau wasn't a fully fledged human to me. He was a haircut with muscles. If I knew how human he was, maybe he'd stop invading my masturbatory scenarios. "What did you do over the weekend?" I asked.

"Much of the same: errands, laundry. Except I work Saturdays, a cycle boot camp class and a core exercise class." He no longer watched me and seemed to check the weight rack for dust. "I, too, read a book."

None of what he said humanized himself to me. I bet he had an impeccable bachelor pad that smelled of fabric softener and aromatherapy. If I saw him at the grocery store, I'd find his cart full of vegetables, chicken breasts, and eggs. I bet his sphincter is so toned, he never farts. I asked him what he read, expecting *Hair Architecture for Himbos*.

"*The Naughty Mommy*," he replied.

If I *had* a mouth full of water, it would've wound up all over the rubber floor. Instead, I wobbled out of an easy-going, body-weight squat. This dude confused me. He was Captain America with the occasional James Bond urge to say the raunchiest thing possible. Was he flirting with me? I rolled with the idea. "Interesting. What's it about?"

"A woman of a certain age realizes she has quite a few things to learn."

"Yeah? Like what things?"

"It's in the title. Naughty things."

"But like what things?" I was really glad that my dark running shorts and sweat were enough to hide how his coy boy routine soaked my panties. At this point, I'd hand him my credit card and tell him to book me for infinity.

His deep, puppy-dog eyes had a hint of amber when he said, "Oh, you know. Bad, bad, things. Egging, TP-ing, forking. I mean all sorts of depraved shenanigans."

I bit my lip to fight my case of blue ovaries until his voice lowered to a rasp. "Put the weight in your heels when you lower and keep your hips back."

The breathy command reminded me I was doing some body-weight squats into a calf raise. The only thing that changed with this conversation was that I'd probably start making unabashed eye contact with him after a session with the Ole Reliable. *That's right.* The next time I flicked my bean, it was not going to be with the shame of using some misconstrued helpful hints imprinted into my spank bank.

"You need to flatten your upper back. May I touch you?"

I nodded.

"Hold your squat."

I paused into the squat, resting my elbows between my knees.

He poked the spot in my middle back again, which rolled my shoulders to attention. With the lightest touch, he pulled my hips back. "Feel the difference?"

I closed my eyes, my breathing shallow. I nodded, unable to vocalize at the moment.

"Good. Now let's add some weights."

Adding weights was a shitty idea. My muscles easily pooped out using them. As I struggled through a set of goblet squats, I asked, "What made you become a personal trainer? Were you a total jock in high school or something?"

"I actually played intramurals in high school. Way more fun and less pressure."

"Why personal training then?" I dropped the weight and took a sip of water during my wait time between sets.

"I wanted to become a physical therapist, and this was the next best thing."

"Hoping to work on some professional team and get that pro money?"

"No. Not that it would be a bad gig or anything. I wanted to be a physical therapist after my car accident." He lifted his joggers and revealed scars from his shin to his knee on *both* legs. Why I hadn't noticed until then I'd chalk up to novice workout navel gazing. "A distracted driver ran me off the

freeway. My legs were crushed. A physical therapist essentially got me to walk again. I thought if I
could do what he did for me, I'd be fulfilled."

My body relived my own painful memories of
inside the hospital. The stupid gowns that tied at
the back, piercing of needles, the scars, seen and un-
seen. "How long did it take for you to walk again?"

"Like I do now? A couple of years."

"I'm sorry. That must've been really painful."

He laughed. "It was."

"If I stub my toe, I don't want to get out of bed.
Worse pain than that? I couldn't imagine."

"There were definitely days I did not get out of
bed. Days when I cursed those who I thought were
luckier than I was. But I reframed my thoughts
and shifted my priorities. That's why I never want
my clients to think they can't do anything. Because
they can. Now let's try a split squat with weights."

My quads were going to burst. I never hated a
movement more, the dreaded split squat. I was on
a descent when Beau hit me with a sucker punch
of a question. "Why do you have two last names on
your registration form?"

I saw what he was doing there. If I was too distracted trying not to murder my quads and hamstrings, I couldn't dig too deep in my brain for some

feeling-sparing excuse. "Front-desk Fran insisted the name on my form match the ID."

"What Front-desk Fr—you mean, Margie? Romanian deadlifts. Eight reps. But why?"

"No offense to the last name Garfield. I love lasagna and hate Mondays, but my original last name is so much better." I switched back to those dreaded split squats again, struggling against my weakness.

"When you say 'original name,' what do you mean?"

Back to Romanian deadlifts. "I'm divorced from Mr. Garfield."

His face twitched as if he was considering something. "Put the weights down, let's do some lunges." Once I was in a rhythm with my lunges, he asked, "What happened? If you feel comfortable sharing."

I was in the midst of a skater lunge, feeling a tightness in my groin, which justified why people bought Hitachi massagers for muscles instead of pleasure. In a front right lunge, I considered how things drifted to feeling more like a roommate situation with Chris a couple years before the inevitable. Holding the back, right lunge, I knew the sexier answer is he left me for someone else, which was the kind of juice that might pique Beau's interest. Shifting to the right skater lunge, I realized the answer might make me seem bitter. Unlike the cliches that were common in the divorced backwash of suburbia, my husband actually left me for a woman two years older than me. And I wasn't bitter... at least not anymore. "Eh, we grew apart." As I said it, it dawned on me I was meeting a boundary I simply did not want to cross. His question was invasive and far too personal for day two of training. He couldn't get me to forget my quads were ready to riot that easily. "It's what I'm comfortable saying."

The switch from the front left lunge to the back one had me joining the pantheon of gym grunters. I might have to go to a confessional after this session. *Forgive me, Father. I'm a gym grunter.* It had never occurred to me that people grunted from feeling the burn, not simply by being some obnoxious bro. "What about you? Any romantic wounds?"

"No marriages. A few break-ups but currently no romantic attachments." His sweet eyes twinkled.

And that was when I realized I wasn't just having a lady boner over Beau Bishop. I was in a full-blown crush.

Chapter Six

I didn't expect this whole goal of storming up a flight of stairs without losing my breath was going to end with me lying in my bed like a starfish groaning. My muscles ached, and any movement needled the individual fibers. A hot shower and a fistful of ibuprofen down the gullet ensured my body system was in survival mode, but I limped my way through work, stretching and craning my

limbs. No satisfying clicks of my joints brought relief.

I returned home after a stop at the drugstore for
some topical pain reliever. The mentholated goop
stung my nostrils and eyes, but I smeared it everywhere, making careful work around my sensitive
areas. Soon after applying it, I washed my hands
to remove the burning layer of cream. The tingling
of my skin served more as a distraction from my
achy muscles rather than any healing of them.

A quick internet search suggested I alternate ice
and heat. I dug some frozen vegetables and fruit
out from the recesses of my freezer. I knew those
good intentioned purchases would come in handy
someday. Bonus! I uncovered some frozen waffles
with only the slightest degree of freezer burn.

With frozen peas under my calves, green beans
resting against my hamstrings, the unfinished
bags of mango chunks and okra plopped on
my quads, I lay in my bra and underwear on
the floor of my living room. Maybe when these
things thawed, I should eat them—when I gathered
enough energy to make dinner.

Then the tingling rose from my stressed quadri-
ceps, creeping to my groin. No worries, it needed
relief too. But then, then, then!

My pussy was on fire! Oh, for the love of God and all that was holy! The nettle-like deep burns attacked my vulva.

I waddled to my bathroom and desperately scooped handfuls of water from the faucet to splash on my stinging crotch. Water only reignited the burn.

I scoured my medicine cabinet for relief. Huh, allergy medicine, the drowsy formula. Not exactly a fix, but it was at least something.

After I popped a dose of the allergy pills, I drifted off to sleep while eating a waffle. Hopefully, the muscle cream wouldn't singe my genitals off by morning.

Boy was I due for a rest day.

Despite the aches and stiffness from five days of training, like the degenerate I was, I craved more. So, I ditched my weekend uniform of PJs for leggings and a T-shirt of a squirrel holding a pile of acorns. It read, *My Nuts are Often Ignored.*

I geared up for Beau's core class. This studio room was empty of spin bikes. Instead, rows of thick rubber mats were surrounded by random piles of exercise bands, a small ball, a weight, and a disc. I located my pile of workout junk in the back corner, where I could sweat and fail in peace. Settled in, I proudly put on my red shades.

The earlier boot camp class finally filed in. The room became noticeably stinkier as the perspiring pain–addicts found their spots at the mounds of plastic exercise doodads. Beau entered, still with his headset on but his body glowing like a god from sweat. He eyed me in the corner. "I see we gained some people in addition to our wild boot campers."

I wiggled my red sunglasses, using the arms at my ears like a lever. *Hey! Beau! Look at our inside joke!* At least I smiled. Beau didn't even react. A familiar shame rose within me. The dinner parties where Chris winced and shook his head at my pithy quip. Moments in which I attempted to enter conversations with the other wives like a game of skipping rope and missed my chance. I slipped the glasses off and set them by my mat.

Some of his perspiring fangirls interjected a *woo!* Seriously, they couldn't help themselves. Dogs barked. Birds chirped. Over–exuberant suburban women wooed.

The background music was relatively inoffensive. The brand of secretary pop rock that moms across the United States tolerated on their top forty

like Coldplay, Lady Gaga, and some one-hit won-
ders who aped the Dad Rock of the 1980s.

We started off holding a plank. He studied the
class in the mirror. "Beth, keep your bum down. If
this is new to you, feel free to do the modification."
I looked around as I held my breath, attempting to
stay up on my arms and toes. No one in the room
did the modification, and I wasn't ready to look
like the asshole who needed to do something on her
knees. My lungs glitched. I forgot how to breathe
as my abs tensed and a muscle in my lower back
pinged. The longest minute of my life passed.

"A good round of planks, team. Let's move to our
hands and knees."

On all fours, I kept my gaze on the front part of
my mat, to avoid studying the too-good-to-be-true
curve of Beau's ass. He did a move called cat and
cow. On cow, his butt flexed up, and I decided to
add that to Ole Reliable's orgasmic memory bank.
Still on our hands and knees, he guided the class
through some single arm and leg lifts. Honestly,
this core class was just my speed. We finished with
some crunches, and for once, I didn't feel like the
learning curve left me behind.

"Excellent warm-up, friends. We're now going to
do some Russian twists. If you feel you need it, use
the exercise ball to prop your back as you twist."

No one in the room used anything to prop up their back.

"Lean farther back and squeeze your shoulder blades together, Sir. Your upper back is curving."

The A-student in me looked in the mirror and adjusted my spine just so. And—wowee—that set my abs on fire. I tried to twist and floundered.

"Don't be afraid to use the exercise ball. It is better to have good form than try something that isn't working out for you today." He ordered us to take a fifteen second break to sip water and recover. I already threw my head to the ground in child's pose to give my tight core a stretch. My shoulders creaked and snapped as if my bones were a haunted Victorian-era building.

"Next we'll do some single-leg V-ups followed by a hollow body hold."

I took a moment to lie down and look at the others. Fun part of the core class was how much lying down could be camouflaged by some core workout. I attempted a V-up. I had never felt my abs give this much of a shit about anything. I collapsed on the floor and sighed.

"Breathe with the exercise. Breathe in as you lower, out as you contract your abs."

I had been holding my breath. How are these other people breathing while also "activating their cores"? Then I ended up doing the opposite. I breathed out as I lowered and in as I reached for my feet.

"Remember to *sync* your breath to your movement."

All of Beau's corrections were coming for me. Dude, didn't beginners get some kind of break?

From the cockles of Hell came the hollow body hold. The squad of matching Lycra women held their bodies in perfect V's and smiled.

"Awesome work team," Beau said as he, too, seemed to have an Olympian set of abs.

I sputtered and rocked, trying to keep my arms overhead, my legs straight, and my lower back from yelling "No bitch!" and giving up entirely. I breathed like I was about ready to birth a baby. I moved my arms to support my thighs.

"Keep your arms overhead!"

That fucker. Did he know it was easier said than done?

Finally, I earned another break. I flopped down on the mat and stared at the ceiling. The fluorescent lights glowed and formed star-like optical illusions in my vision.

"Back to V-ups. Right now!"

My abs hurt. I didn't have it in me to touch my toes. Flat on my back, I raised my legs at a forty-five–degree angle and weakly reached up with one arm.

"To get the benefit, you really need to lift your shoulders off the mat. Way to go, Liz, you're getting it."

I wished *I* were Liz. Instead, I looked like a cockroach, my limbs weakly reaching toward the ceiling.

"Alright, we made it through our first set. Two more to go!"

This had to be a joke. My effort in the second set dwindled considerably. How was everyone else in the room armed with abs of steel? I thought America had a fitness problem. Not in the gyms of Gorda Vista.

When I couldn't feel more incompetent, Beau announced, "We're going to hold a shoulder stand. Remember to lift with your abs and flex your gluteal muscles."

Beth swung her legs up above her head as if she were light as a feather. Oh, the benefit of having one of those narrow heart-shaped asses. In contrast, my ass had heft. I swung my legs up, but my ass was still grounded, and my boobs were now trying to smother me to death.

"Shoulder stands are difficult. To modify them, you need a couple of bolsters." He disappeared into a closet for a moment and brought out two giant pillows. He plopped one next to me and the other at his station. "If you place a bolster at the small of your back, you'll still get the workout." He demonstrated the pose with the pillow underneath his back.

But there was Beth, her tits not trying to prevent her breathing. Her matching Lycra-clad tiny ass defied gravity.

"There is no shame in using the modification. We are all built differently," Beau announced to the class, but it was definitely directed at me and my ugly, grunting face.

I started from the bottom and then rocked my legs all the way back. I held my breath as all I saw was my T-shirt in my face.

"If you swing your legs, you're not practicing good form."

Jesus, Beau, I got it. I was Shitty Shitterstein of Shitonia. I would never taint the progress of this core class with my presence ever again. I would've walked out had Beau not announced we were about to complete our final set.

At the end of class, we had to put all the supplies back into the closet. The bootcamp crowd talked about how their abs felt activated. I aimed to throw everything in the closet and bolt.

Then Beau, as if he was my damn fifth-grade teacher, said, "Sir, can I talk to you for a second?"

What could a himbo have to tell me about my abs? I sidled over to him. "Yes?"

"Why are you selling yourself short?"

"I don't know what you mean?"

"Your effort. Don't you know you're worth giving one hundred ten percent?"

"One hundred is the maximum. One hundred ten percent does not exist. I couldn't do those moves. I'm pretty sure this core class isn't for me."

"It is foundational to your success to have a strong core. Once you have a strong core, everything else falls into place, cycling, strength training, even walking will improve. Do you get back pain?"

Not often, but now that he mentioned it... "Not all the time."

"You owe this to yourself. When I see you again on Monday, I want to see a concerted effort."

"Okay." Jesus, Dad. I hadn't had anyone be disappointed in me since the divorce.

Effort? He wanted concerted effort?! I'd show him!

After class, I stormed off to run my errands, needing a few items from the store. In my frothing anger, I did a weird thing. I parked my car at the back of the lot to get more steps in despite my stomach muscles twisting about angrily. *How's that for effort!*

Arriving home, I rage-put away my new pack of toilet paper, peanut butter, and box of crackers, slamming my cabinets shut. Now what? My foot tapped; my leg bounced. I wasn't necessarily demonstrating that I was down for opening a spicy book and putting my feet up.

I kicked open the door to my office, now mainly used for storage. Hands on my hips, I assessed what to do next and shoved unpacked boxes off my drawing table. As soon as I plugged in my digital tablet, I took a deep breath, raised the stylus, and drew. Lines, squiggles, curves all flowed from the electronic pen. In the rush of inspiration, I illustrated a cockatiel riding a bicycle—completely unrelated to recent events. What inane statement captures the aura of a bicycle-riding cockatiel? *Free beak rides.* Perfect. This was probably the level of satisfaction DaVinci felt painting Mona Lisa's smile.

I returned to sketching my twisted characters, the ones that polluted my failed business: possum, raccoon, cat, and the new addition of the cockatiel.

By Sunday, I had a new file folder stuffed with images. Yet an energy still sizzled through me. I stepped out for a walk, blasting Britney Spears in

my ear buds. I even walked near the EverGreen
& Fit Studios, sort of wanting to see the follicular
skateboard ramp shadow in the darkened windows. Once I confirmed no classes were in session,
I walked right into a post of the map of businesses of our downtown area. On the announcements
side, I discovered a neon pink flyer. Preeti Sun-
daram, a graphic artist who I followed online, was
doing a book signing and Q & A session at the cute
little indie bookstore, Crooked and Booked at the
end of the month. She had completed a graphic
novel for kids.

Whenever I had seen an artist succeed the way
I never did, my first reaction was "That sono-
fabitch." It was in a pleased grandpa way, which
challenged the notion that artists didn't do deluded
things like "make a living off our craft." The me of
about seven years ago, freshly thirty, tried to take
my goofy art to the next level with silly merchandise. That version of me went to book signings and
talks. That version of me handed out postcards of
my art with QR codes to my social media accounts.
That me was killed with silence and stored in boxes, then two boxes, and finally one box in the corner
of my condo. And when I encountered the artists
who drew more important things, had better state-
ments to make, I stopped handing out those post-

cards. I stopped discussing craft and color theory because I wasn't one of them. I was a desperate dilettante, a hobbyist, a dabbler. I was going to live the rest of my life putting my artist's eye to use by designing corporate things. How many artists could at least say, "I'm designing *something*"?

When I took the photo of Preeti's flyer, I had no plan to do anything with it. A photo was just a photo, a brief amusement about the success of a fellow artist. Scratch that. For I was neither fellow nor artist.

Finally, the torrent in me calmed down, and I read my book in bed. I flipped the page and heard the whispers of "concerted effort" echoing. A smile pulled at the corners of my mouth. I had drawn, walked, taken care of myself. I couldn't wait to show Beau what one hundred percent—nay 110%—from me looked like.

Chapter Seven

At the start of personal training session three, Beau asked, "Did you lose the red shades?"

"Didn't feel like wearing them today," I answered. If he expected me to give 110%, I could no longer hide behind the red tint.

We put in a thirty-minute easy round on the bike. My T-shirt, a rainbow-colored chameleon labeled *The Only Constant is Change* stuck to the sweat on my back.

"You're not getting enough power on the bike because your legs are tight. We'll focus on your lower body today."

Focus on my lower body? He'd have no arguments from me.

He put on a track of some chimes ringing over and over again to make the stretch session more vibey and relaxed. I bent over, giving my legs a slight bend to graze the ground with my knuckles.

"Move from side to side to release the tension in your back."

I swayed like an elephant swinging its trunk. The tension in my lower back relaxed.

"Now roll up carefully, vertebra by vertebra."

I popped up. No big deal. Was this the worst Beau could throw at me?

"Slower. You're moving too quickly. Try it again."

I folded myself over again, with the slight crook in my knees to relax my arms. He stepped behind me, the tip of his sneakers only a few inches from my heels.

"Can I touch you?"

I nodded. Though naughty mommy ideas of those sneakers wedging between mine and his long fingers digging into the full part of my hips entered my mind. I gave my pelvic floor a preemptive squeeze at the idea.

Instead, he put two fingers on either side of my spine right above my coccyx.

"Really imagine your body in a *C*. Hollow out your abs, exhaling. Now roll up."

I flexed my glutes and tipped my tailbone down. His fingers followed my spine. "Do you feel the difference?"

A part of my back clicked loudly into place, announcing my age. His fingers walked up on either side of my furrow. "Roll your shoulders, move your blades toward your spine as you move up."

His fingers were now at the base of my neck. I lifted my head into place. My eyes slowly opened. In our reflection, my gaze met Beau's penetrating one. I shifted, rubbing my thighs together and licked my parted lips.

"Feel more aligned?" he asked.

I was feeling something alright. I nodded, but I was in a daze. That was the Beau Bishop effect.

His gaze followed my body from head to toe. He was checking me out. Did I, Sir Hooper, possess the desirability of my decade-younger self?

Ooh la la. Yeah right. What was so enticing? Gravity's pull on my boobs, which dropped bit by bit every year? The newly emerged "hormonal gut" which granted my belly even more of a curve? No, Adonis-like personal trainers were monitoring

form, which sometimes resembled checking someone out. I needed to tell my brain and my neglected
libido to chill.

"Get on all fours," he rasped.

Wait... wh-what?

I dropped to my knees, locking eyes with him as
I moved down. If he was going to bring a naughty
edge to these sessions, I was at least going to project
the same energy right back. Two could play this
game.

He met me on the mat, parallel to me.

"There are a few lower body stretches I like doing
from here. First, we're going to do a cat-cow. It's a
yoga move we've done before. It helps stretch your
core muscles, and you find equilibrium with the
curve of your spine. If you like being a good girl and
receiving extra credit, you can tuck in your toes and
get a foot stretch out of this as well."

He had me at good girl. I had to bite my lip as he
modeled, and I mirrored him, stretching my tailbone and chest up, cow, and then curling both down,
cat. I attempted tucking my toes. Yowzah! My foot
arches felt like they were being pulled apart. Un-
tucking my toes, I settled for regular credit and
being a regular ole woman over being his good girl.

"Do a few more for me." He jumped to his feet
and seemed to study my body flexing, as if I was

some sort of mammal presenting herself to her alpha, and he watched the C's my tailbone drew in the air. "In cow, push your shoulder blades together. In cat, push through the floor and find the room between your blades. Your back will thank me."

I completed one more cat–cow, trying my best to incorporate the pointers. My back muscles loosened thanks to Beau's expertise.

He dropped to the mat and demonstrated some stretches to help release my psoas. Next, the calves. He showed me how easily he lifted his body into a downward dog, stretching his calves by reaching his heels to the floor as his hips angled up and back.

"If you bend your knees a bit, you'll feel where your hips need to be to get the most out of this position."

I did what I was told.

"Straighten your legs. Now, hold it."

He slid behind me and his hands went for my hips. *Holy shit.* He tugged them back. "Good. Keep your hips back. Your shoulders are lifting up too high. I find if I treat my arms like rope and imagine them twisting, my shoulders find the right position."

I followed the word picture. My weight distributed itself equally among my fingers. The pressure on my index finger was the same as on my pinkie. My shoulders found more space in this position, and my hips slid farther back—closer to him.

"Good. Now I like to walk my dog, meaning I pedal out my calves." He scrambled back down to his mat and demonstrated what the hell he just meant. Shifting my weight from calf to calf stretched my legs inch by inch. They were tight. *Really* tight.

I sucked air through my teeth.

"Is it pain or is it discomfort?" he asked.

I breathed in and out. "Discomfort." I experienced a similar feeling twenty years ago when I had sex for the first time.

"Then your calves really needed this. Listen to the chimes. Breathe, relax into the stretch."

I didn't disappear into the music. I lingered on the memory of him pulling my hips back to him.

"Sir?"

I shook myself out of my stupor.

"Lie on your back," he said.

Sometimes I wished I were less polite. I'd tell him his orders are hitting all the wrong parts of my brain. I was not recognizing an instructor honed in on improving my physical fitness but a fellow dirty mind taking me down a whole other path of physical fitness.

He handed me a yoga strap. The timbre as it dropped to the ground sounded like a loosening belt buckle. He stretched out next to me, causing another anticipatory twitch of my Kegel muscles.

"Leave one leg straight and raise your other leg like so."

He lifted his leg, again at a perfect ninety-degree angle. What was it about exercise and ninety-degree angles? He placed the strap under the ball of his foot and pulled the ends. With the help of his arm strength, he lowered his shin toward his face. He grunted, obviously finding discomfort. "This is one of my favorite hamstring stretches."

I expressed the equivalent of the meh emoji. How could anyone have a favorite stretch? Particularly one that seemed to be digging into the minutia of my muscle fibers and eking out any bit of pain.

He rolled to his knees and stood up at the end of my mat. "Can I help you straighten your leg? One hand would be on your ankle and the other above your knee."

"No objections from me."

He kneeled at my feet and did as he said. What I wasn't prepared for was the warmth radiating from his hands that sent so many embarrassing sensations up my thigh to sizzle below my belly. Frankly, he was not charging me enough for these sessions. The pressure he put on my leg was light, helping achieve a deeper stretch.

"You don't want to force it when someone helps you stretch. Tighten the hold on your strap."

I pulled the ends of the strap, gathering the fabric inch by inch. He let go of my leg, and I maintained the length he had helped me achieve.

"Other leg," he said. Strangely, breathy and low.

I lowered my stretched leg and lifted the other. I looped the strap around the arch of my foot and pulled the ends of it toward my shoulder, gathering the excess in my hands. His hand met right above my left knee to straighten my leg. I gasped.

"Good?"

I blinked and nodded, inhaling and exhaling through the stretch. If this was as close as I could get to Beau, I could die a happy woman.

Soon the hamstring stretch was over. He showed me a couple more moves—something for the IT band that combined the concepts of horrendous and orgasmic. Opposing forces contributing to my restoration or blah blah blah.

"Honestly, I could see myself using these moves into old age," I said as I packed up my gym bag.

"I'm glad to expand your horizons."

"I should put on the Yelp review *so good you'll need a cigarette afterward*." I laughed, expecting

him to join in, but he narrowed his eyes. That immediately put my giggles on mute.

"Was that a sex joke?" His eyebrows expressed
all the shock.

I lowered my gaze. It would take me another
swipe of my credit card to buy the time to explain
all the innuendo he let pass, and I mistakenly in-
terpreted the vibe. Got it, keep the pervy shit to
a minimum. "Yup." I popped my *p*, to make my
shame linger.

His face relaxed. Sweet little crinkles surrounded his eyes. "Good one. See you tomorrow."

I had it bad. Why did I prepay?

Chapter Eight

B eau was like WD-40 for the soul.

A newfound rush of horniness combined with stronger muscles and stretched out limbs made me in need of company. So, I threw myself to the wolves with online dating.

I downloaded a dating app to assess the area dick on demand. I set up my profile, having to find a good balance of photos. Everything I had was almost three years old and required me to crop out Chris. Disembodied hands in dating profiles didn't bode well. I needed a fresh set but didn't have the social calendar of someone who did cool things like attend cocktail hours, concerts, lie out on the beach, or hike. But I could pretend to be. A shower, shave, and a round of teeth whitening strips later, my mission began.

First photo, I went to my condo's poolside. Posing in my sunglasses, floppy hat, bikini, and holding a real margarita with a fake daisy in it, I fidgeted on a lounger at the pool as if I was on vacation in Cabo. Between my props and the sunshine, all that was missing was sand, relaxation, and eighty-degree weather. I was settling for a cool fifty degrees. With enough pool chairs and pillows, my phone sat at an angle where I could manage something flattering. A hundred shots later, I discovered the pose that emphasized my boobs and the pool. Ronald and Florence from the condo down over stared confused from their perch on the hot tub. I'd edit them out in post.

This next one took fewer props but way more effort. I hiked up the Caballero de Hierro Trail to the picturesque top of it, the town of Gorda Vista below. Winter brought enough moisture to the area, so the normal rocky and dusty terrain came alive with rolling green hills and fields of orange flowers. With a few rocks and twigs, I set up my phone and propped my foot up on a boulder.

For the final photo, I had to go for something journalistic. I assessed the decor in my condo. My kitchen, with black granite counter tops, was open plan and blended within a few feet into my living room. I kept my furniture simple: a comfortable beige couch with a similarly plain easy chair, which held every blanket I ever owned. My bedroom had a similar plain yet comfortable style. I added color with my rainbow-hued pillows and framed art of my favorite illustrators, Eric Carle, Maurice Sendak, and Lizabeth Zwerger. My living situation needed to tell a more active story. I dusted off some Christmas decorations, laid out some fake evergreen on my fireplace mantel, and put on an old sequin, cocktail dress. With my hair and make-up on point, I leaned against the mantel holding a half-drunk glass of red wine. I didn't have to fake the half-drunk part. I faked a laugh as if I heard a good joke and *click* took a photo. A couple more glasses of wine, I found the perfect "in the moment" photo.

With the impeccable dating profile of a cool woman, I scrolled through the menfolk offerings: awkward selfies, a sentient sunglasses and ball cap holding up a fish, a posed photo with a disembodied hand. Didn't anybody make an effort? I settled for

swiping right on an awkward selfie. Half a bottle
of wine later, I finally had a match and a message.

> *Hi pretty lady*

Eye roll. I typed.

> *I see you like to travel :) Where have you
> been?*

Unmatch.

Eventually the effort of the day and the wine and
margaritas took over. I was half passed out in bed
until I heard a vibration. A match—one of those
disembodied hands people.

The match sent a message.

> *Heyyy*

> *Chilling and reading a book :) What are
> you up to?*

> *Watching Netflix ;) What are you reading?*

First one set the standard so low, I was already
feeling heartened by this match's art of small talk.
I wasn't going to scare them off with the real me.
What important books in my library had I not
managed to read?

> *The Testaments :D What are you watch-
> ing?*

Ah, a Booker prize winner. Rewatching Mindhunter.

Shit, I reeled in a cultured one. I speed-read some Goodreads reviews to help if he quizzed on my knowledge of Margaret Atwood's latest.

Then he sent another message.

Your photos are cute.

Thx ;)

I added to my response.

Mindhunter is a good show :) Too bad about the cancellation :(I enjoy the work of David Fincher. There's a cute indie cinema in Clarktown I'd love to go to sometime.

DTF?

Wait what? My finger hovered over the block button. I hesitated. Maybe I could mine this situation though and get an easy lay out of my system, so I wasn't so damn awkward around Beau. This could be good for me. Heck, maybe this—I read, Ryan from Chestnut Grove—would be good for me. We'd discuss books, prestige television over drinks, and address our horny issue.

I could be… >:) After a couple of dates

He sent me a photo. I tapped it and saw a dick pic, a thumb–looking thing in a mountain of tangled pubic hair.

Block button.

But all wasn't lost. I had another match. The match messaged.

> How are you doing?

> Great! Chilling at home :) And you?

> Not so well. Didn't respect my dairy aller-gy lol Now I'm stuck on the can.

Huh, not the kind of vulnerability fit for an intro-duction. I hit *Unmatch*.

Maybe getting on the dating horse was going to be a lot more difficult.

Chapter Nine

A few weeks went by in which I was prepaying for one-on-ones and flirting surreptitiously with my personal trainer. When I ran out of actual alien romance titles to talk about, I made up my own, *Bend Over* and its sequel *Touch Your Toes*, a political commentary on the tax code and polyamorous relationships. Beau recommended a series that were fictional retellings of getting into the Olympics, *Hard* and *Wet*.

In addition to my workouts, Ole Reliable was getting put to so much use, I bought it a companion piece, *Georgia*, a pink monstrosity that sucked and shook at such a level it was obscene.

Wrung dry from working myself out all morning, I ended up walking to the Saturday farmer's market in search of fruit for my oatmeal. I was now regularly eating an easy, high-protein oatmeal recipe Beau shared with me. It tasted amazing with fresh peaches, apples, blackberries, or whatever else a farmer's market offered. As I skipped between the stalls, overpaying for some peaches and still quaking a bit from Georgia's erotic pulses that accompanied thoughts of a cockatiel-like hairdo between my legs, I goddamn ran into Chris.

When I moved into a condo and Chris and new wifey took over our old home, I was bound to run into them outside of a lawyer. The slice of suburbia we had settled in was Chris's hometown after all. He probably expected me to go back to the Midwest with my tail between my legs, but I had a job and life out here too. It just wasn't that stellar of life or job. But they were mine.

At least Chris's forehead gained more real estate since I last saw him. His light brown hair receded farther back. Some of that stress weight he put on during the divorce had worn off as well, so he appeared as gangly as he did the day I married him. Of course when we were married, he wasn't wearing the Gorda Vista middle-aged man uniform: button-up, puffy vest in navy or black, hiking jeans, and top siders.

"Sir," he said because he couldn't bother to say, "Hello."

"Hey Chris. Have you tried the white peaches around the corner?" Spreading some of Beau's enthusiasm was what an unexpected conversation with an ex needed.

"I'll tell Claire we should check it out." Claire was the woman he left me for. Not the fairest statement about him because our marriage was withering on the vine, and he knew Claire before me, being high school sweethearts and all. When we went to the twenty-year high school reunion, they had one of those amazing heart-to-heart conversations that reminded them of all those things they missed about each other. And—I loved this for them—they had the bravery to explode two marriages over it. Neither cheated in an intentional, physical sense. They took a high road of brutal honesty. It was just hard being on the receiving end of brutal.

Chris's gaze seemed to bounce around the people at the farmer's market. That meant Claire was about, and we were destined to have a meeting of the wives. Maybe I could weasel out of here quickly enough. "Well, this was delightfully awkward, but I got—" I pivoted right into Claire. Claire, in all her Sarah-Plain-and-Tall glory, the human embodiment of the BRAT diet of bananas, white rice, unsweetened applesauce, or white toast. And Claire was very, very pregnant. Not a normie woman wearing an empire waist outfit, mistakenly seen as pregnant. Waddle and heartburn pregnant.

"Hey Sir." Claire rubbed the top of her belly, right where it protruded from the bottom of her ribcage.

"Wow, Claire. You're—"

"Pregnant. About six-months along." She glowed.

The ground dropped from under me. I was in free fall, grasping the injections and mountains of negative tests that littered my past life with Chris. Prickles of the heavy sadness arose from those memories. I took a deep breath, feeling my eyes sting a bit.

"Congratulations. That's so great!" I put a hand on Chris's arm. "I know how much you wanted this."

He nodded.

Claire smiled; her gray eyes narrowed. "You look really good, Sir. Happy, even." She trailed off a bit at that last part. The last few years were miserable, but the worst part was knowing we were miserable because of stasis. I hadn't had the words or bravery to leave my marriage. Marriage meant I had a sure place to stay and at least one set of eyes on my stupid cartoons. And the abject terror of filling out divorce papers and realizing I didn't have a place to call home anymore, that the eyes who looked at my stupid cartoons were full of indifference? Yeah, I probably didn't look happy then.

But I was happy now because... because...

"Welp, as I said, I gotta go." I swung my bag of peaches and pushed myself into a full sprint. I wasn't going to my condo but toward the gym.

I burst through the doors, scanned my membership card, and rushed through every room of the studio. If I was going to work out, I'd be one of those weirdos someone would upload on social media, wearing ripped jeans, a sweatshirt with a dead possum on it titled, *Self-Care: Play Dead.*

The cycle bootcamp class let out. The last to file out was Beau. He was toweling himself off. Sweat darkened his green tank top and weighed down his silly hairdo, and of course, it was so damn beautiful like that. His eyebrows raised when he recognized me.

"Tell me if this is out of line, but this Thursday evening there's a book signing and author Q & A at Crooked and Booked, and I wanted to see if you'd go with me." This was a situation where words came before thoughts, and now that they all left my mouth, I ground my teeth because his answer was definitely going to be "I'll refund this prepaid week."

"Okay. When?"

"Right, that's what I thought." *No, you dumbass, he just said okay.* "Wait what?"

"When on Thursday?" He draped his towel over his neck and ran his fingers through his hair.

"Oh. Seven? Should I pick you up or..."

"I don't live too far from downtown. I can walk and meet you."

"I don't live too far from downtown either." Beau and I could have easily crossed paths before the gym. Maybe we had, and I hadn't noticed because he was the age and level of attractiveness that I blotted out before. Solar eclipse man, too bright, so I looked away immediately.

"Meet there?" he asked.

I nodded.

"Get drinks afterward or is that—"

"Yes. Yes, we can get drinks afterward." I embarrassingly had far too much enthusiasm, wafting eau de desperate.

"It's a date."

Hearts flew from my head. I had a date with Beau Bishop.

Chapter Ten

I ran out of the shop on Thursday, to get a head start on date prep. I shaved, showered, deep-conditioned the hair, buffed the body of dead skin cells, applied toner everywhere, and oiled up. I was going to be the best version of me.

Then came the hard part. What vibe was I going for? If I wiggled out of here in a cocktail dress and fuck-me heels, I'd have an orthopedic issue by the end of the night and would stick out at a damn book signing. So how do I go straight for the middle—relaxed but also looking like I was putting in some effort but not so much effort that made me seem like I was a teenager on her prom night?

I chose my Doc Marten boots, tights, a circle skirt, and a fresh screen-printed T-shirt of my recent cockatiel drawing. I layered a flannel over it to add a nonchalant air.

The frosting to my shit cake was my makeup and hair. I had about twelve minutes before I needed to go out the door because I spent too long worrying about my outfit.

After I ran a brush through my dryish hair, I sprayed a little root blender on my new growth. The aerosol can farted out the last drops of red before the spray fully covered my roots, so I smeared a bunch of burgundy eye shadow on my silver roots to do the coverage job that my hairstylist should've done last week, but I'd been too much in a Beau haze to remember to schedule an appointment.

I checked the time and had fuck all left. I smeared enough of that same burgundy eye shadow to fill in the brows I over plucked twenty years ago. In my defense, pencil thin brows were in at the time, and I didn't know they wouldn't grow back. Finally, eyes. A little swipe of some going to "land me in the ophthalmologist's chair if I don't throw it out soon" mascara would make do. I lined my eyes with the globby end of the wand and blended the line with my pinkie. Sure, I had nice brushes, but they were shoved at the back of the drawer, and I was not getting those in the two minutes I needed to leave the condo.

Since I was not using an applicator or a brush, my eyes looked a bit racoonish, but it was a smokey eye. And raccoons were the kind of animal that embodied my soul—dexterous hands, tubby bodies, a penchant for eating garbage. Claiming smokey eye since 2001 covered up the fact that I never really learned how to do eye makeup. I misted on some setting spray and was ready to go.

I jogged so I could make it to the bookstore on time, arriving in a far too moist condition for a date.

A man was waiting outside the bookstore, but he was in no way Beau. This guy wore a pair of clunky boots, baggy jeans that fit his hips well, a corduroy jacket, and some Rivers Cuomo–looking, horned-rimmed glasses. Maybe Beau was inside?

I nodded at the guy as I pulled the door open to the store.

"Sir," the guy said.

I stopped. Did I know this man? Then the recognizable shape of his shoulders and swoop of his hair hit me. "Holy shit, Beau. I didn't know that was you." I hadn't seen him without green athletic gear. What's the opposite of Lois Lane's situation? Where she has the hots for Superman but ignores Clark Kent? Dammit. That was the word for it. Because dammit, what Beau in glasses did for me.

He held the door open for me. "Want to do this?"

Inside the store, we settled into some plastic chairs. With the presence of some elementary-aged kids, I suddenly grew self-conscious over wearing a cartoon oral sex joke across my chest. I buttoned my flannel.

"I thought it was funny," Beau said.

"You think all my shirts are funny."

"I know."

Preeti, from head to toe, was dressed in a rainbow of colors: bright purple cat-eye glasses, a yellow blouse, green cardigan, and a purple-blue flowered skirt. She paced the front of the room, handling a microphone hooked into a tiny speaker, as if it were her personal karaoke machine. Her speech accompanied a slideshow. One slide showed the first drawings of her career, which had developed into her independently produced animated series. Another slide consisted of the latest from her graphic novel.

To a layperson's eyes, her cartoons went from cute to cuter, but I noticed how even the plump sausage cartoon hands improved, how her shading gained more depth. I sat forward in my seat as she demonstrated to the excitement of one of her new and young fans how she drew a dragon. "Curved lines and dots," she said. "One at a time."

I bought a copy of the graphic novel *Captain Capybara and the Golden Sloth* and held it to my chest. I scanned the short line of people, mostly children, getting Preeti's signature inside the front cover.

"You should get her to sign your copy," Beau said.

"I'm not a kid."

"You don't have to be."

"You wouldn't want to wait in line with me. We should—"

He stepped in line and gestured to a space in front of him. It wasn't his fault that he didn't know I felt a little fraudulent around real artists.

I made it to the front of the line and handed my book to Preeti. The quickest possible way out was to go through the motions.

Peering over her giant purple glasses, she asked, "Whom should I make this out to?"

"You can just sign it. I'm sure your wrist hurts."

"Saoirse," Beau said. "Make it out to Saoirse."

"S–A–O–I–R–S–E?" Talented artist and knew how to spell names that didn't appear like they sound? Goddess.

My ears turned hot. In a stroke of her pen, I was absolutely not worthy of breathing the same air as Preeti.

"She's an artist too," Beau chirped. "Drew that cartoon on her T–shirt."

"Really? Can I see it?" Preeti's eyes beamed from behind her glasses.

I sheepishly unbuttoned my flannel and exposed the freshly screen–printed bird on the bicycle.

Preeti leaned forward and muttered the words underneath it. "Free... beak... rides?"

"Yup." It wasn't lost on me that Preeti's grandiose project was a novel that enriched the lives of children. I wrote T–shirts that made Beau giggle. I was the fraud in an artist's clothing. Why did amusing my smirking companion supersede common sense?

"She has other animals too. Possums and cats," Beau, the effervescent source of *not making the situation better*, added.

"And do those animals ride the bird's beak?" Preeti's mouth gaped, quite possibly in the horror of it all—cartoon interspecies orgies. But it was a level of world-building I hadn't thought out. Me, ever-the-pantser of an artist.

"I think... they keep it between birds." I winced, but then a lightning bolt of inspiration struck me. "But who knows what happens in that dirty alley behind the free clinic." I should seriously stop yes-anding this situation.

"Best of luck to you and your art, Saoirse." Preeti handed me the signed copy.

"Thanks." I couldn't run out of Crooked and Booked fast enough.

The ever-pounding run of a clunky booted stride trailed after me laughing. The little ding of the door of the bookstore also was thankfully behind me.

"I think I'll go die now," I said.

"Maybe you could've broken her in with the possum or cat, but I'm sure she'll never forget the bird."

"I want to forget the bird."

"Where are we going next?" An eagerness lit up Beau's face.

"This was the plan. Now I guess we will go home."

"No, no, we are *not going home*. Not yet." He swiped the book from my grip. "What did she write to you?"

"I'm sure it was 'Thanks for coming!' or 'Appreciate the support!'"

He angled the book toward a streetlight. "Ride that beak, Saoirse. Squeeze with your thighs and don't let up on life until it passes out."

"That is not what it fucking says." I reached for the thing like I was a teen girl in a mean game of keep away.

He tucked the book in his back pocket, the gargantuan kind that came with vintage jeans. "Drinks like you promised. And I'll give you your book back."

That was how we ended up in this chic cocktail lounge, where they have freaking vinyl bound menus with a gold embossed logo to add to the glamor of it all. The place was named Vine and Spirits because the building grew a lot of ivy all over the front. I kept my gaze fixed on the menus, trying to decipher the drinks and their strange names. What did I begin drinking after a book signing on a Thursday night? Chamomile tea?

"What are you thinking of getting?" Beau wiggled in his seat to the beat of the jazz music playing in the background.

"No idea. You?"

"Espresso martini."

"Ugh, no. I have to work tomorrow, and I'll be up all night from the caffeine."

"I have a cycle boot camp class at six a.m. tomorrow, but I figured I could be a little bad tonight."

"At your age, you can make bad decisions and spring out of bed the next day."

He tilted his chin in the air. "At my age? How old do you think I am?"

I couldn't be old enough to be his mom. Maybe his older sister or former babysitter. "I'm thirty-seven years old."

He squinted his eyes at me. In disbelief? Or confirming the bags under my eyes and the sprinkling of silver saying I'm desperately in need of another visit to the salon? "I'm twenty-five."

"So, I could've been your babysitter."

"Sadly, you were not."

Before I could lecture him about how problematic it was to fetishize the babysitter and the babysat, the bartender finally made it to us and asked for our orders. I gestured for Beau to order first—to stall until I made up my mind.

He swiveled on the barstool so his knees met mine. Nudging my knee with his, he said, "C'mon Sir. Be a little naughty with me."

My spinal fluid hit reverse. "Make that a second."

"Two espresso martinis." The bartender brewed espresso, flipped a shaker, and shook it with such gusto, I couldn't tell if he was angry about the order.

"I thought you were worried about the drink keeping you up all night," Beau said.

"It will. I better have something good to do." A beat passed between us. Our flirtations up until then seemed like jokes, a game of chicken until one of us finally pulled away. I pressed my knee back against his. I was going full throttle toward him, foot firmly on the accelerator.

The martinis arrived. We both took sips, but I loved how the froth stuck to his pronounced cupid's bow on his lips. He had to lick a droplet away.

I took a gulp of my martini to help myself ask this next question. "Why are you single?"

"Are you asking what's wrong with me?"

"I've been trying to figure that out since I've met you. You said no current romantic attachments. So do you have any war wounds?"

"You're assuming that matters of the heart actually deal with the heart."

His answer felt cryptic. "They don't?" I asked.

"A lasting relationship relies as much on the brain as it does the heart."

"So much wisdom for a youngin. And you're being coy." I gave the bottom rung of his bar stool a playful kick.

He sipped on his martini again. "Women find me attractive."

"No shit."

"And I've dated, but I've never been someone's first and final choice."

I took another sip of my martini and raised my eyebrows, as in *well, what does that mean?*

"I tend to be the rebound." There was no usual smirk or glow in his eye as he said it.

"Give me an example."

"I'm good at helping the women I've dated find what they've been looking for in someone new or return to what they were running from."

"So, you're a fixer who doesn't pick the right ones."

"They feel right enough at the time. There're just some aspects about me that they weren't comfortable with."

"Are you a werewolf? In a religious cult? Were you somewhere you shouldn't have been on January sixth?"

He shook his head and laughed. "We live in an area where a lot of people are very educated, and I didn't finish college due to the accident."

He rubbed the top of his thigh. I saw horrific flashes of seeing someone so athletic and put together mangled in metal. I stilled the hand on his thigh. *The past was past,* I wanted to say. *We were not the things that happened to us.* But like the reticent old lady like I was, I said it with the touch of my hand. He sighed.

"What's stopping you from going back to school?"

His smile became a little forced, maybe even sardonic. "It probably missed me at this point."

"You're still young."

He shrugged. "You lit up when she discussed her drawing process."

"It was kind of brilliant how simple she made it all seem."

"But you got so hesitant talking to her. What's going on there?"

"Did you see her drawings? They were *paintings!*"

"I like how yours always come with a little commentary."

"I'm not on the same level. Did you hear how many drawings she went through before landing that illustration gig? I've never had that level of discipline ever in my life."

He fished the graphic novel from his back pocket and placed it on the bar. He opened the front page and pointed to Preeti's message.

Saoirse, from one artist to another, you captured his likeness well. Ride that beak. Preeti.

Preeti outed my fuccboi cockatiel as Beau. She wasn't horrified by the horny bird. She *got* it.

He brushed the placket of my flannel aside to get a better look at my T–shirt. Staring right at my tits, he studied the cartoon. "Now that she mentions it, I'm seeing a likeness, except my hair doesn't stick up that high."

Obviously, his back was to the mirror during cycle class because it was that high. But I drew it when Beau was a distant fantasy to me, when he was Superman.

I asked the bartender for a pen and swiped a clean cocktail napkin from across the bar. "If you want to be a physical therapist, you should be a physical therapist." With some arcs, lines, and dots, I captured his jawline, aquiline nose, brilliant eyes, and his silly hairstyle. With a few more swoops, I added his broad shoulders, strong legs. "If not for yourself, for those who need to know there's still something to the second act." Adding a bit of shading—the kind one can do on a cocktail napkin and ballpoint pen—I finished the cartoon but not before doodling a speech bubble and a few more accessories. The cartoon Beau held a foam roller under his armpit, had a rubber strap draped over his neck, and presented a model spine like it was a trophy. The speech bubble said, "Your spine is fucked."

I slid the napkin over to him. "Put that on your vision board."

He huffed out a single laugh and tucked the napkin in the pocket of his jacket. "You want to get out of here?"

I nodded. We finished our martinis.

Outside of the cocktail lounge, he took my hand into his. "I have a roommate."

"Of course. It's the only way anyone can afford to live here." I squeezed his fingers into mine, an auto response. He said *roommate* because he wanted to take whatever was going on between us inside, to be alone. My body thrummed at the possibility. "I don't. Have a roommate, that is."

He smiled, tiny. Unnoticed if one was uninitiated to his quirks. Genuine, not his stupid customer service one. "So, we're heading to yours, then."

We forged ahead, making small talk about how close we lived to the bike trail. Bemoaned that the area neighborhoods had an unfortunate lack of streetlights. Living in Gorda Vista, we weren't exactly worried about a criminal lurking in the shadows, but some coyotes had been spotted. *And fuck if I'm getting rabies from a coyote.*

Beau gestured vaguely toward a cross street we walked by. "I live over here."

"Never thought the NIMBYs would allow apartments there."

"No, I have a room in a house. A generous step up from a cardboard box."

"You got a real room and board thing going on. How very nineteenth century." I laughed, imagining Beau as a Mr. Bishop who seduces the governess with his vim and vigor.

"Amenities include a basketball hoop in the driveway." He broke away from our hand–holding and mimed shooting a basket, jumping, and cheering at an invisible three–point shot.

I caught myself with the widest grin watching him be an utter goofball. He had to have noticed because he stopped. "You have a beautiful smile."

Damn, a compliment. How should I respond to that? Thank you? You too? "Tell that to my dentist," I replied with a snort. Ah, sarcasm, the shield I needed when Beau set his charisma protons on faze.

I spotted the gray rows of condos that were my place. "I live in a condo, in case you thought I lived in some Real Housewives of Suburbia monstrosity. My ex-husband and his new wife bought me out of my former house. He's my landlord, the ex. Bright side? I got rent control." I had been trying not to talk about Chris and Claire because they were in my past. And tonight's date wasn't about them, I lied to myself.

"What's your roommate like?" I asked, mainly to distract myself from the ex-induced negativity spiral.

He stopped and drew out cloth to clean his glasses from the pocket of his jacket. Cleaning his glasses might have been the sexiest thing I had seen him do, and I've watched his ass move in Spandex. "Older, clean, super nice, pays the rent on time, but it's not exactly a panty dropper to say, 'I have a roommate.'"

"Women want to drop their panties just looking at you, so consider your roommate situation panty neutrality."

We arrived at my front step. I was in the midst of coping with the idea that—holy shit—he'd see my living quarters when he leveled me with, "What do I do to your panties?"

I froze, right foot on the top step, left still on the bottom. My arm crooked at an angle in preparation of putting my key in its lock. "Things."

He touched my elbow. "What kind of things?" I pivoted to look at him, stepping up to the top step. His left eyebrow quirked above the rim of his glasses. He closed the gap between us, but he stood on my bottom step. The top of his hairdo lined up with my chin.

Holy shit, we might kiss. Holy shit, we might dry hump. Holy shit, we might get naked. Holyshitholyshitholyshit. My hands shook, confirmed by the jangling of my key chain. "Beau? The last time I did anything remotely like this, I was married to him."

He kissed the top of my hand. His lips were warm in the cool night. "I'm a big fan of baby steps."

"Of course you'd have a perfect answer."

He did that lean in where he was definitely going in for a kiss.

"Beau?"

His lean stopped, his lips hovered only a few inches before mine.

"Let's say we get carried away, and we don't baby step. I'm not on birth control, and I think if I found any condoms in my junk drawer, they'd be expired." Not at the bitter end, but Chris and I were trying to have kids, so it was strange to return to this part of my life that avoided the outcome of sex.

My heart hammered in my chest merely thinking about all the baggage that came with sex and babies and no babies.

He held my face in both of his hands. "We haven't even kissed, Sir." He ascended to the same step as me and went for it. I no longer blurted the words produced by my current anxiety loop. He opened his mouth slightly and sucked on my lower lip. It had been years since I'd been kissed like that. Embarrassingly, my knees buckled, and I stumbled into him moaning.

"I'm kind of lousy at this." My sinuses stung while I forced out a nervous laugh. Making out on the front porch was supposed to be a happy occasion. Why was I going weird and vulnerable?

"I'm sure it's like riding a bike."

"You *know* I'm lousy at that."

"Then we should keep practicing." He went in hard and deep, his tongue sliding across mine. I gripped his neck for dear life. His kisses were going to kill me. Once we had a good thing going with our tongues and lips, he grabbed me by my waist, his thumbs gently grazing around my bra line. "Why the fuck aren't we inside?" He smiled and a stray kiss of mine went for his teeth.

Because with the way things ended with Chris, kissing and groping might as well be the equivalent of the Moon Landing, one giant step into the unknown. And then my brain went Chris Chris Chris Chris. Our sex became so clinical that I didn't even think we kissed when we initiated it. Ovulation, work schedules forced it. Books and blogs told me to fake it until I made it, but all the faking meant sex felt more like picking my nose. How very unsexy. The sex was with no kisses and barely any eye contact, in which I noticed a water spot in the ceiling and not the man over me trying his damnedest to get me pregnant.

And then my mind twisted and turned to those times when I sat on the toilet, staring at the giant blood spot in my underwear, begging it not to be real. The first one sort of shriveled me for a while, but I read the literature, I went to the therapy, I said another time will be different. But again and then again. *It* stopped being devastating and just a fact.

Saoirse couldn't have babies.

I turned the knob of my front door, my heel backing into the threshold. "Why me?"

Beau short-circuited and was stuck on an "Uh-hhhh..."

"Apart from you getting a kick from attempting to clear cobwebs out of my vagina. Why me? I'm just—"

"You're great."

"I'm broken. You're trying to fix me and make things okay, but maybe I'm fine being broken. Have you ever considered that?"

"You're not—" He lurched forward probably for some stupid kind of hug.

"I can pay for your Uber home."

His mouth fell open. "No. That's okay." He stepped off my stairs and paused on the sidewalk out of the cluster of condos.

"It sucks now, but I swear, Beau, I'm saving you from your pattern. I'd be another person you'd try to fix."

He nodded and walked briskly into the dark, where the coyotes lurked.

Chapter Eleven

I ghosted Monday's session, then Tuesday's. After the middle of the week, I grew antsy, missing strength training and cardio. It was not like Beau owned the place. If I full-blown stopped showing up at EverGreen, I'd be doing some immature avoidance. I didn't need to avoid Beau; I just didn't need to flirt with or fuck him. Easy. That was practically the status quo. Me, invisible to the twenty-somethings of the world.

I returned to the gym halfway through the week, thinking my radio silence was a strong enough message. I wore my raccoon shirt and vintage neon orange Zubaz pants. The raccoon sat in a trash can, wearing a takeout box for a hat. *So trash I'm someone else's treasure* scrawled at the top.

While I grooved to some No Doubt, in a traditional squat using the free weights, I felt a brush on my shoulder. I removed one ear bud. "I got about five minutes on this set." Even I was impressed by how gym lingo tumbled out of my mouth.

"Sir?"

I took a moment to study the person poking me. Perry. *Claire's* Perry. When both our marriages went up in flames and Chris and Claire rose from the ashes, Perry took it the hardest, lawyering up and fighting every little thing along the way. In comparison, I had more warning when my marriage had flatlined because, according to Perry's version of events, he and Claire were in love until that high school reunion. Chris was some evil interloper. And honestly, it was a little hilarious hearing my saltine cracker of an ex-husband described as some other man's antagonist.

"I wouldn't have recognized you without the pants. I didn't know you worked out... here."

"Yeah for almost a month now." I kept the other earbud firmly in my ear, not even bothering to pause my music. New Saoirse Hooper was serious about her reps.

"Want any pointers?"

I sighed. The real answer was no. I had some pretty good personal training. On the next inhale, I was going to chuckle and say the Midwestern, "Yeah... no." Then behind Perry, about ten feet away, I saw Beau wiping down a leg press machine. He sprayed and wiped the same spot. A trainer should tell him to relax his shoulders; that was only going to lead to upper back tension. And really, brooding and eavesdropping? Not a cute look. Okay, not *that* cute of a look. Our suburban enclave wasn't that big, and if it meant I had to avoid certain locales or behave a particular way not to upset the *two* people who once had interest in me, I could only travel between condo, work, and the hair salon that dyes my silvery brown hair burgundy. Know what? Poor Perry. I'd play the part of a clueless woman to give him some balm for his bruised ego.

"Sure."

He grabbed a massive set of free weights and racked them on his shoulders. His face was already turning red from apoplexy. "See how my shoulder blades are drawn together?" Sure, but maybe if he had a better personal trainer, someone would tell him he needed to size down on the weights and time his inhales and exhales based on the contracting and releasing of his muscles. I watched him squat, and he spouted something about knee alignment that I already knew.

"You gave me something to consider." And I added one of those weird fake laughs, the ones that moms use when their kids scream *Watch me!* and they do something silly or unremarkable.

"Have you seen them lately?" Perry asked. By them, of course, he meant Chris and Claire.

"Yes, actually. At the farmer's market about a week and a half ago."

"So, you know that she's..." He patted his dad bod belly.

I forced myself to smile wider and nodded.

"What do you think?"

I thought I was going to barf. My insecurities were laid before me in Claire's pregnant glory. Chris never said it because he was a grown-up, but the implication was always there. He ran back to his high school sweetheart because she had a scientifically proven reproductive system. Mine was a complete failure. *I* was a complete failure. But I wasn't going to unload all that on Perry. After all, I felt Chris and Claire characterized me as *the one who took it well.* "Good for them. I've been so busy, I don't think much about them anymore. I've been working out, drawing more, starting to see the town at night for once."

"I suppose you have it easy without a kid." Perry gazed off into some unknown area. Did I mention Claire and Perry had a kid? About nine years old. And they named him after a character in a Tom Cruise movie like Jack, Maverick, or Ethan. I couldn't remember. As I said before, Claire had a proven functioning uterus. And Perry now had a proven record of bringing up all my sore subjects in the duration of a five-minute conversation.

I checked over my shoulder. After Beau practically wiped a hole in the leg press chair, he conspicuously adjusted the pin on the weight and tested the machine with his hand. A small smile crept across his face, as if he learned that no one on planet Earth was jealous of Perry.

"How are you doing?" I asked, hoping Perry would quit prodding the wounds of my soul.

"You know. Good days. Bad days." His posture sunk, his face falling into the most pitiful frown. He wiped sweat off his forehead.

He truly had a way of getting people to feel the pathetic part of empathetic. "Have you ever cycled here?" I asked.

He shook his head.

"There's a cycle class tomorrow after work." And before anyone could mistake me as a trifling little bitch, I added, "Starla teaches it." Truth. I tracked the classes Beau taught and specifically attempted to avoid them this week. One of the other instructors, Starla, was even more *Woo!* and way less artful with the double entendres, but lithe and athletic Starla had something more going for her than the previous instructor. She hadn't made out with me. "You could join me."

"I don't have Maverick tomorrow." He paused to calculate. "Yeah. I could do that. See you then." He went back to breathing terribly through leg day.

I honestly forgot which rep I was on. I was about ready to put my earbud back in.

"Who was that?" a voice behind the overhead press asked. Beau. I'd recognize the plume of hair over the top of the machine from anywhere. The world was conspiring to get me not to see the end of these reps.

"My ex-husband's wife's ex-husband."

He parted one of the weight plates to view me on the other side. His gaze danced from side to side as he mouthed husband, wife, and husband again. He tipped his chin when it dawned on him the connection between Perry and me.

"So, you have a lot in common."

On the surface, yes, but if Chris was a saltine cracker, Perry was a soggy, salt-free variety. Back when Perry and Claire were together, I was sure the flies on the walls in their home died of boredom. "Not exactly."

"Did he offer you any good tips?"

I slammed the weight plate down. Honestly, if it pinched one of his lovely long fingers, I'd have no regrets. I swung my head around the machine to look directly at him. "Are you spying on me? I thought men your age were raised on the internet and knew to knock that Cro-Magnon shit off."

"You were a no show," he shout-whispered through clenched teeth.

I pointed a forceful finger in his direction. "Go find another desperately horny middle-aged woman. I'm sure if you tell her you'll 'light up her loins' with a bike ride, she'll hand over her credit card."

"No other woman wears such ridiculous pants."

"Oh yeah?" I pulled the saggy pants out like I was curtseying. "You like 'em? Good luck finding a pair!" I forgot we were shout-whispering and turned the volume up to a shout-shout. "I thrifted these. As in one of a kind! Unlike your fuccboi shtick."

"I'm not a fuccboi."

"Well, tell that to your haircut." I stormed out of the place. Once I had made it halfway to my car, I realized I could stop marching in a huff. I turned the engine on and Bluetoothed my phone into my car radio. Before pulling away, I finished the song that had been grievously interrupted.

I punched the ceiling and rubbed my newly chafed knuckles. I just wanted to do my reps! As I pulled out of the parking lot, I promised myself that after tomorrow, I needed to find a new gym.

Chapter Twelve

I spent the morning designing a series of test business cards for a professional tree-trimming business. He wanted a redwood in full-color and toyed with raised print matte or gloss so I made a few for comparison, providing that one-on-one service only a local store could offer.

He liked the matte finish with the raised print because *everyone* likes the matte finish with the raised print, and his competitor had the shiny business cards. He wanted to be, and I quote, "a cut above the rest." I couldn't make this shit up.

I quoted him the price for a gross of his beloved cards.

"I can get it cheaper if I order it online," he replied.

If I had a nickel every time I heard that.

"I'm not sure online can offer you a unique design. You say you want to be 'a cut above.' Online is going to offer templates everyone else uses, imprecise printing and cutting, and a glossy sheen that reeks of 'I undersell my work.'"

"Can you do a price match if I find something similar online?"

No way, dude. Between my boss and me, we had mouths to feed. And I had to save money to sign up for a new gym. "I assure you, we are priced competitively. As a *local* business, we know how hard our neighbors are working to make ends meet. And so are we." I laid on the guilt. That would do it.

He ran his fingers over the raised pine needle detail in the corner. If I hadn't peaked at a possum cartoon, tree-trimming business cards might be my magnum opus.

"What's the minimum amount I can get?"

I sold him a box of 500. I guilted him enough to reward my hard work with the minimum amount, the story of my life.

Tina emerged from the back. "Got a sale. Good for you." She drummed her fingers against the counter. "Saoirse, I've been putting off this conversation."

I didn't work for Tina for almost a decade without knowing the direction of her conversations. She was having to pull the drawstrings of the business ever-tighter as more and more local businesses printed their crap online. I knew when I accepted the job working for The Mighty Pen Printers that I was working for a dinosaur circling a tar pit. But it was one of the few jobs in Gorda Vista that at least applied my background in art and design. The last time a conversation began like this, I threw myself into my ItsyBizzy store, hoping I might break into entrepreneurial success. Alas, a few boxes of merch had collected dust and Chris's ire.

"I'm thinking of running the shop exclusively online. Turn this place sort of into a showroom by appointment. Which means, I might be reducing your hours here and, consequently, making pay cuts."

Without having to pay for hormone injections and other pregnancy treatments, her news was way less soul-crushing than it would have been a few years ago. Unlike the other washed-up creatives polluting the area, I had an agreeable landlord, and until I ever remarried, I had that sweet,

sweet alimony for a few more years anyway. I had a backup and a plan for survival to claw out of the tar pit. The wine and paint store a few streets over could use a teacher of drunk women painting sunset landscapes. I could do my part in being exploited by the gig economy. This was life in the tar pit when society devalued art but still demanded it. "You have to put food on your table too."

"And it may be just offering a lousier health insurance plan or—" She stopped and stared at me. "You're taking this very well."

What can I say? My current cardio regime made it harder for my pulse to get worked up.

As if by cue, my sister sent a million texts to my phone. Apparently, Mom joined an adult tap-dancing class at the senior center.

Good for her.

But she got into an argument with the instructor over the choreography.

Of course.

Now Mom was never going to return. And Fiona had to listen to Mom complain over coffee about how she still had zero friends to go shopping with.

Yeah, Mom, stop being mean.

And Fiona would have to go with her to go to an arts and crafts expo because Mom was crying.

I texted back.

> If I send you fifty bucks, will you get me the ugliest thing you find at the expo?

Not the feedback she was looking for. She left me a message that was prime evidence my potty mouth was genetic and not something born from my personal dysfunction.

I showed up fifteen minutes early to Starla's class to claim two bikes in the cool kids' row. Workout outfit: overpriced bike shorts and matching sports bra set I recently bought in lavender. The T-shirt? A cartoon raccoon and cat frolicking in a field of catnip, a detail missed on maybe the one keen observer who also noticed there was a pile of cat toys behind the raccoon. The message scribbled over the scene? *I could play with my pussy all day.* Not a metaphor for the sex toy arsenal I currently possessed. In my defense, Chris thought it was hilarious until I wore it to a dinner party. A few art experiments and a chemical burn later, it became an unintentional crop top.

The design might work up Perry. He'd be the type to say I couldn't wear something like that in public, the kind of adult that Chris eventually became—or maybe always was but was less fearful to express near the end of times. And frankly, I wanted Perry to sputter and sweat so hard, he'd regret ever interrupting my reps!

I warmed up on the bike, and more people arrived, to the point where I had to insist that the bike next to me was reserved for a friend. I suddenly grew self-conscious over whether the *friend* would show up, or I would look like the asshole in the cool kids' row, reserving a bike that everyone wanted.

Perry finally arrived, wearing the standard dad workout wear: practical white shoes—the ones that hadn't been ruined by mowing the lawn—white crew socks pulled up past the shin, compression shorts layered under dark gray cotton ones, and a navy T-shirt for a 5K charity run that happened two years ago.

He mounted the bike. I stopped him to adjust the seat and handlebars just like I'd been taught and repeated how he should roll his shoulders back, keep his back flat, push his hips to the fat part of the seat, and engage his core. And like the me of the recent past, he did practically none of that and needed a bit of hands-on coaching. Light, barely touching hands because Perry—gross.

We got a good warm-up going on, and then a voice boomed over the speakers. "Hello you party animals. Starla is sick, but I got a good ride for you today. Who's ready?"

Beau. As in rhymes with *O*. As in *Oh shit*.

Hey brain! Come up with an excuse. My shoes are too narrow. That's the ticket.

I reached to touch Perry's shoulder to gain his attention. "My shoes—"

"Woo!" Perry forced a high five on me.

Dammit, I couldn't leave now. I'd be the world's biggest jerk if I snuck out and witnessed that dopey little grin of his deflate. I shifted back onto my seat and began pedaling. Beau stared daggers in my direction.

"I'm Beau Bishop, and we're going to get hot and bothered. This evening's theme will be taking off our clothes. But you don't have to if you're not feeling up to it. In fact, that big knob between your legs can add resistance if you turn it right. If it's too hot for you, you can always take a little off by turning it to the left." Beau mounted his bike front and center in the room. "We got some runs, some climbs, and yes, I will hit you with some HIIT but only with your consent. First," he said, swallowing the mic, "a little foreplay."

Christina Aguilera's "Dirrty" played over the speaker. I rolled my eyes.

"This guy is funny," Perry said with a chuckle.

This *guy* was insufferable.

During the warm-up, Beau talked about how he was a toddler when Britney and Christina kissed Madonna on television. He polled the class to see if we were more Britney people or Christina people. The class split evenly. Some even conversed over the music about their choice, as if they were in a serious geopolitical discussion. *I dance more to Britney. Christina can belt!* The next song was "We Don't Have to Take Our Clothes Off." Beau announced a medium climb.

"I understand if we're feeling a little sheepish. Add more to your resistance. You might be putting on more, but things are getting harder. Get out of your seat and climb."

If I could stand on my pedals and slowly clap for his performance of the year, I would. My quads and hamstrings were primed for the worst to come. And like damn clockwork, the opening chords of Nelly's "Hot in Herre" roused the class into a chorus of cheers. I had to take this personally. I'd be deluded if I didn't. Beau glowered straight at me.

And like someone who had to keep their chest forward, bum back but not arch their back, I was torn between wanting to slap him or mount him like a bicycle.

Fine. I cranked my resistance to the highest range he announced and picked up my pace to match his. It was going to get hot, alright. The chorus kicked in. "Bring the sweat, can you take your speed to 100 to 120!"

My legs vibrated to the point of jelly, whipping those pedals around. I was going to 130, hitting a personal best purely out of spite.

"How do you do it?" Perry grunted and wheezed.

"Sing to the music. You'll start breathing better." I panted out the advice as sweat poured into my eyes.

Then Shakira's "Underneath Your Clothes" kicked in, a flat road track. "You don't want to give it your all yet. Take this moment to drink water, wipe yourself down with a towel. We do get a little messy when we're excited."

The major climb track arrived with a brutal contrast to Shakira's ballad, Methods of Mayhem's "Get Naked."

"Take a look to your left and a look to your right. We're all going to get closer by the end of this ride.

Share some intense intimacy as we get absolutely filthy."

My thighs burned as I pushed through the molasses-like resistance. I was full-blown mouth breathing, tasting the iron of my unconditioned lungs.

"Remember to breathe through your belly. If you remember to breathe deep, I can take you to your limit, make you feel things you never have before." He growled that out. I'd like to say after that there wasn't a dry seat in the room, but of course, we were sweating. Scowling Beau tingled over my body, practically zinging right to my clit.

He wanted to play games? He got it. I whipped my sweaty shirt off. I had ascended to a new level. The brave woman who wears nothing but a sports bra and shorts to the gym. I pretended to have to adjust the straps to give my boobs an extra bounce.

Beau licked his lips. "We're going to try some choreography. To the beat of the music, you are going to touch your butt to your seat and pick it right back up, aiming your hips toward your handlebars." He ran his fingers through his sweat-soaked hair. "Show me what you can do with those hips." The entire class hip thrust back and forth to the beat of the song. At this point, Perry kept himself firmly planted in his seat and leisurely pedaled, rocking the something is better than nothing philosophy.

The next song in the cavalcade of millennial perversion continued with Ginuwine's "Pony." Beau smirked, peacocking for everyone in the class. "I know what you're thinking when this song plays." He stood up on the pedals and lifted the hem of his shirt to show off his Adonis-like abs. One of the ladies in the front row almost tipped her bike over in a frenzy, as if Beau was a boy band member.

Maybe that shit would have excited me a month ago when I believed glimpses of him were all I could get. But I knew he could do better. I toweled off, dragging the terry cloth over my cleavage, tit for tat. Or more *tit and tit.*

Lowering his shirt, he directed us to push through another burst of cardio. My heart thundered in my chest. The blood in my body zig-zagged in my veins. Should it go to my limbs or to my aching pussy?

"Give it your all. Those limits are white noise. It's just you and the music, baby. You got this! Yes! Yes! Yes! Good girl."

I braced against the handlebars and bit into my lip as a moan escaped my throat.

The music changed to "Versace on the Floor." Beau's voice lowered. "We're on the other side. We need a cool down, a stretch, a shower." He led the class through a stretch.

"I'm Beau Bishop, and I'm subbing for Starla. I hope you have a good night."

Father Fuccboi took us to church and got the women to speak in tongues. I was a quaking puddle of a human being.

"Do you want to go somewhere after a shower?" Perry asked.

I waved a wet noodle arm in his direction. Waiting for the ability to use my limbs like they were supposed to work was the consequence of pushing myself to highest resistance and speed. I panted out, "I made plans after this." Not quite a lie. Putting on a deep conditioner mask on my hair and slugging my face with all sorts of salves and creams was on the docket. He didn't know how flexible an activity I had planned.

"Right. That may have been too much excitement for one night." He wiped down his bike, coating the dark spots of sweat with a green solution. The gym should mention it was also ever-good at its branding. Perry held the two ends of the towel, which was draped over his neck. He looked up into the fluorescent lights above wistfully. "Thanks for suggesting this, Sir. I needed it. See you around."

I nodded.

Members of the class thanked Beau on their way out, Perry among them. Beau nodded breathlessly, smiling through the endless line of gratitude. I finally gained enough command over my body to retrieve the cleaner and wipe my own mess off the bike. I shuddered, the response of someone feeling watched. And I was being watched. Beau frequently broke eye contact with the dwindling throng of fans to linger his gaze over me. Maybe that was why I slowly left the bike. Not some lactic acid buildup or a need to cool down, but rather a desire to feel the pull of his thrall. His puppy–dog eyes became more—what do they say in my romance books?—like orbs of lust.

He gathered towels and wiped down bikes that still had marks of sweat. I dismounted from my seat, draping my crop top over my neck. I smoothed over the sweaty tendrils that had stuck to my face like tentacles. "Is Starla actually sick?"

He shrugged and moved from row to row, grabbing stray towels, which he off-loaded into a cloth hamper near the exit.

"Seriously, Beau, what was that class?"

He took off his mic pack and earpiece. "A bit of fun." The way he wiggled out of the band which held his mic excited me. The way he could have taken his pants off in my bedroom if I hadn't completely chickened out. "Didn't you come with a friend?"

I followed him into the storage closet. He put his mic pack on a platform to charge. "Friend is even a little generous," I said. "We went through a shitty thing together. We're like war vets nodding across the room together. We *know* why we have the thousand-yard stare."

"You were smiling."

"I'm Midwestern. I've been raised to believe it's my job to smile at people."

"I'm in customer service. I know a customer ser-vice smile when I see one. And you *smiled* at him."

"Are you twelve? I'm not the one preening and glistening to get the attention of sweaty middle-aged people. I'm smiling? You essential-ly fucked a whole room without actually fucking them."

He grabbed the ends of my shirt as if pulling on a bridle and crashed his mouth into mine. I tripped into a rack of small weights. He licked inside my mouth; I responded by sucking on his tongue. I tasted the salt of his sweat and swooned, taking a few weights with me. Directing me with my makeshift harness, he pushed the tiny one-pound and two-pound weights aside. The divots for the weights prodded into my ass. He broke away to slam the closet door shut.

The anxiety loop threatened to return. "Beau, we—"

He put his fingers to his lips to shush me. "I don't want to listen to reason. I just want." He embraced me, his hands rubbing the small of my back. "Don't you? Want?"

His thigh rubbed right at my apex. The friction made me mindless. Marching from the aerobics class in the next studio thundered through the closet walls. As if the universe was aligning, the pop song demanded that I *take a chance*. You know what? Fuck it. "Yes. God, yes."

I sprang up from the rack, and we staggered into the dark of the closet like a couple of teenagers playing Seven Minutes in Heaven. Lit only by the light shining through the crack under the door, I shoved him into another shelf of workout doodads. He sat back on a giant yoga ball. With the height discrepancy, he buried his face in my chest, licking at the sweat of my cleavage.

"I'm so sweaty and stinky." Not exactly the paragon of sexiness.

He squeezed one boob and nipped at the other through the Spandex of my bra. "I fucking love it."

I took fistfuls of his sweat-soaked hair and held his head against my chest. Salt, the raw smell of him drove me wild, as if I was trying to hump him on a yoga ball.

His touch glanced at my inner thigh. "Can I touch you?" He traced his fingers along the outline of the V of my crotch, right across that needy nub of mine with only a centimeter of fabric stretched over it. "Right here?"

"Yes," I breathed in his ear.

He struggled at first with the tight fit of the Spandex but dipped his hand past my waistband. His skillful fingers parted my seam and mixed my sweat and arousal together in strokes.

"I knew you'd feel like this. That you'd get so wet and ready for me."

"Mostly sweat, you cocky—" He tapped my clit, and I whimpered.

He tapped a few centimeters to the right, then the left, a dull but wicked sensation that nudged me to the edge.

"I'm a cocky what?" He didn't wait for an answer, his fingers went for it, straight for my clit.

I clawed at his back, finding next to nothing to hold on to as sweat slicked his skin. I lifted the hem of his shirt for something to grab on to. My knees knocked into the rubber ball. "Keep going."

He changed speed and pressure. Just as I dug my fingers into his back, he changed his hand into a hook and entered me. "Ride me like the good girl I know you are."

The pressure was glorious. I cried out and bit into his solid mound of a shoulder to stifle myself. Shit, we were in a closet at his job, and I was riding his hand shamelessly. I got a good rhythm. The class on the other side of the wall quieted down, which emphasized the sound of my stifled moans, the squelch of me fucking his hand, and his heavy breathing. And because he's Beau and perfect, he added a thumb back to my hard bead at the top of my pussy. I was getting massaged inside and out.

"Look at me," he growled. "I want to see that pretty face when you come."

I lifted my head off his shoulder and looked at the shadows of his face. Of what I could make out, the dark cast of his gaze had just as much of a command on the squeeze of my inner walls as his hand. Beau Bishop wasn't just a sunshiny himbo; he was a wolf. I bit down on my lower lip and studied him, his predator glare. I ground my hips faster and faster, and my first duo orgasm in years seized and shook my limbs. I held my lips together so tightly that I frayed my vocal cords to mute the sound.

Never breaking eye contact, he released his hand from me and pulled the band of my shorts back in place. He raised his fingers to his lips, glistening with me, and he sucked them clean. "Delicious, sexy." When he was done with me, he smiled that infuriatingly smug grin.

I kissed him again, sucking on his lips and tongue, tasting my personal tang. Jesus, I knew my way around my lady parts, but Beau found something new. I lowered my hand to the band of his shorts.

"What are you doing?"

My hands shook, as they had when I did not know my way around men's pants. The sterile sex with Chris had put me out of practice. "I'm returning the favor."

He grabbed me by the wrist and twisted it behind my back. "I can't be fucking around at work." He lifted me to my feet and kissed me again. "Shower? Your place?"

I nodded. And I was scratching the hair mask, eye mask, face mask, and tea plans.

That self-satisfied smirk said he knew exactly what he was doing. "Go on now. I'll linger back here a little longer. Wouldn't want anyone getting the right idea. I'll meet you back at yours?"

I opened the closet door. The bright lights painfully shrunk my pupils. I tarried, still wobbly a bit from Beau's magic hands. But something else called me to stay there, as if it was completely natural to want to cuddle after having a mind-blowing orgasm. "Beau, that was—"

"I know! I'll see you soon," he shout-whispered.

I looked at myself in the giant mirror at the front of the studio. I resembled someone who'd spent an hour in the sauna and peed her pants. I draped my crop top over my arm and raced out of the gym to my car.

I hit my head against the steering wheel. My personal trainer had given me the best orgasm of my life in a closet on top of a yoga ball. And now a shower. He was going to shower with me. A laugh emerged from my lower belly and prickled my chest until I sat a whole minute in hysterics. Beau Bishop rocked my world.

Chapter Thirteen

I parked in my assigned carport and ran and skipped to my condo. I started up the shower to make it nice, warm, and steamy. He had seen me, red-faced, drenched in sweat. And honestly, these bike shorts weren't doing my softer body any favors. But he told me I had a pretty face, and it rattled me to my core like I was a teenager. If we were going to have an adult playdate, I needed to feel like my best self, even in the most absurd sense.

I dug out my waterproof eyeliner and mascara to touch up my eyes and put on a little lip stain. After tugging my hair out of its ponytail, I finger-combed it into something—mainly a sweat-soaked mass with a dent in it from my hair tie. I posed for the mirror. His dark gaze etched into my memory as I bit my lip. The way he touched me—my lips, back, pussy. I grabbed the counter, reliving it.

Listening to my shower run and contribute to the desert wasteland of the future, a twinge nestled into my chest. He could've lied. Promised he'd come over only to not. And there was the other side of me that was like my teen self, the perpetual anxiety and disappointment brought on by the masc individuals who I pursued and let me down.

Wine dulled anxiety, so I moved to my kitchen and opened a bottle of merlot. If I drank half a glass with no sign of Beau, I'd take that as a sign to step into the shower alone, not to hope for the eternal affection of a young Adonis and live the rest of my years holding the memory of getting fingerblasted by the prettiest little fuccboi ever.

I lifted the delicate glass by the stem and sipped. Merlot was a smooth, dependable wine. Not too overpowering. I didn't need much to be happy at my age. So what if a twenty-something-year old went back on his word?

Music. Gentle, ambient music was what the situation called for. Anything to gargle out the bad taste in my ears after the naked themed ride. Another hearty sip, I got out my towels and tested the water temperature in my hands. Welp, shower alone. I peeled my Spandex off and—

Ding dong! I snagged a foot in my bike shorts as I bolted to the door wearing my towel. I stuffed its edges under my armpits to keep it from falling to the floor, in case it was some unexpected package delivery. But the video from my doorbell app confirmed, I had a sexy man in green on my doorstep.

I opened the door. Of course, he leaned on the door frame, wearing his Evergreen zip-up jacket and still the messy clothes he worked out in. "I see that I overdressed."

"Get in here. It took you long enough."

"I stopped to get some of these." He took a giant box of condoms out of his jacket pocket. "You said you weren't sure if you had any."

"Well then." I snatched the box from his hands. "Get naked and get in my shower."

My towel dropped to the floor, and he lifted me toward the direction of the shower. He kicked off his shoes in transit and wiggled out of one set of his bike shorts. He placed me on my feet in my bathroom, and I helped him out of his shirt. I stepped into the shower and ran the stream of water over my head and boobs, where it gathered along the creases of my thighs.

Usually when I took a good look at myself naked, I noted the things I could work on or the stuff I would suck out, stitch, and staple if I had the money. When Beau looked at me, I was proud of this body I had spent so much time in. I even found myself peacocking for him, squeezing my tits together and pinching my nipples. "You like what you see?"

He nodded, his lurid stare fixed on my body as he took off his socks and peeled his compression shorts off. He was so beautiful it was unreal. And my pussy pulsed a bit watching his dick move between his legs as he tore a condom from the long line of them. He stepped in the shower with me and placed the condom square on the divot for soap. I let him get the warm stream of water on his head and body. He flicked his hair back, looking like some ruffled feathers of the cockatiel cartoon. "Well then, indeed."

I kissed him a bit too sweetly, and we held each other under the stream of water for a while. Why weren't we immediately going for each other's genitals as we had back at the studio? I wasn't sure. For me, I was saying, with my head nestled in the space between his collarbone and shoulder, that it took a marathon to get here. Not the cycling class or the strength-training sessions, the marathon of a stale relationship, miscarriages, an indifferent divorce, and finally standing here brave enough to be vulnerable again, if I'd ever been vulnerable with Chris.

I stroked his perfect jawline and admired the way the water stuck his eyelashes together. He still was a cinnamon roll, puppy-eyed man, but I liked how he could be a little bit of everything. Brooding, jealous, dark but still be this ray of sunshine for me. Part of me felt he echoed similar feelings—that in this quiet moment before we were going to ravage each other, we were promising not to hurt each other.

His sweet expression turned smug again. "Did I mention I'm an excellent boob washer?"

With a glob of soap, he went straight for my tits, rubbing my nipples until I let out a sigh. He glided his hands over my arms, belly, and back, lavishing me with attention. I bet he cleaned under my nails, but I was so transfixed with how tender he was.

My turn. I didn't want to rush. As a doodler, I simplified the shapes of humans and creatures to a simple curve. The details I tended to smooth over were the best parts, the tendons and veins in his strong forearms, how his eyes crinkled when he smiled, that his aquiline nose had a slight crook to the left, and his smile creased his right side more than his left.

Parts of him were superhuman: his thick trapezius muscles, rippling rhomboids, and the pronounced groove of his latissimus dorsi. I could've aced that muscular system test in biology for non-majors. Because unlike the information that went through one ear and out the other in biology class, I wanted to name all of Beau's muscles. Put a stake in them with my kisses and fingers. I grazed my nails across the small patches of hair on his chest and down to his shallow belly button.

I reached for his cock, and he hissed.

"How do you like to be touched?" I murmured between kisses.

"Anything from you is great," he said almost dreamily.

The piss-taker in me couldn't help herself. He set it up, here came the punchline. "So, I should slap it, scratch it, leave bite marks, twist your balls?"

His ab muscles tensed. "Oh, ho, ho, ummm, no. Unless you really want to?" His brows formed with concern.

"No, but I'm asking for feedback."

"I like to be touched here." He gave himself short strokes right under the tip of his penis. I learned more about him. Beau wasn't circumcised, so his skin moved as he showed me.

"Like this?" I joined his hand and hooked my other arm around his neck. He leaned against the tile wall of the shower, and his Adam's apple bobbed as he swallowed. The water from the shower cooled. I didn't have the water heater of wonder, but the cooling water mixed with his warm arousal.

I kissed the soft spot between his jaw and ear. He whimpered. I felt powerful. "Want me to keep going?"

He nodded, and his head rolled back.

"I'll finish you off like this. Then I'll take you to my bed and give you my mouth and pussy. By the end of the weekend, I'll have wrung you dry."

"Please." His abs heaved, and his mouth dropped as he released over my hand.

I raised my hand between us; he watched me with sleepy eyes. I licked the soft skin between my thumb and index finger with a hint of his semen.

"Did I do a good job?" I knew I did, but I had internalized his praise so much over the last month, I needed to hear it from his satisfied mouth.

"Even in a warm-up, you gut me. You're such a quick learner. Such a good girl."

I turned the now ice-cold water off. "Even I have enough mental clarity right now to know you overdid that." I stepped out of the shower and dried off, taking my sweet time as I really liked the way he looked at me.

I handed him a towel, and he dried and then tucked it around his waist. I combed at my tangles and watched as he ran his fingers through his hair. His coif reached its glorious height with a towel dry and flick back. I loved his stupid hair.

"Am I spending the night?" he asked.

"We take the evening as it goes." I casually moisturized my skin, not the full-on slug I had planned. Beau may have seen my face covered in sweat, but seeing me covered in every moisturizer in the drawer in my bathroom was a Jedi-level of relationship that we were not ready for. Like, yes, he could put his tongue on my ass but see me fully moisturized and face masked? Nope.

"I'm asking because I really need to take my contacts out. I could wait until I get home or—"

"You have to wear your glasses." That Clark Kent thing he had going for him did me in as much as his praise.

He smirked. "You like my glasses?"

"I love your glasses," I replied, unthinking. I'd call that a rookie mistake—how easily I blurted the word *love* in a purely sexual relationship. Yeah, I knew I was referring to an object associated with him. But let's be real, once a person threw that word around, I was not too long from drawing hearts around his name in a notebook. Red nervous blotches spread from my chest to my neck.

Bless him, he didn't make much of it except to continue his smug smile. "I have another problem. I didn't really come with an extra set of clothes."

"You really hurried over here?"

He blinked out a "no-duh."

"I have the perfect solution."

One unpacked box of merch later, we were nestled in my bed—me in the PJ set with cartoon foxes all over it (not one of my designs), him in my high school gym shorts—seriously, the elastic and poly-blend of it was magic—and an unsold T-shirt of mine. The shirt had a duck neck deep into a bottle of wine. Doodled across the top, *Wine not? Mommy has corked up trauma.*

I sat with my back against his chest, his legs bracketed me in on each side. I skirted my fingers along one of the scars on his leg.

"When did the accident happen? You mentioned college."

"Sophomore year. Spring break. I never really did anything wild for spring break—more like went home to save money. I was on the freeway, and before I knew it, the jaws of life were getting me out of the car. I learned a distracted driver switched lanes right into me, and I spun off and rolled over."

"You could've died." I squeezed him a little harder.

"Nearly did. But I try not to think about how scary and lonely going through that was. What got me walking again—got me out of the house—was knowing I lived to breathe for another day. So, I guess that's why I can be a bit... insufferably sunshiny."

"You're the right amount of sunshine." I kissed my hand and rubbed it along his scars.

"Still have some pins in my legs."

"You're a partial tin man with a heart." I put my ear against his chest and listened to his heartbeat. "What were you studying in college?"

"Acting."

I laughed. I could see the girls, boys, and enbys laying themselves down before him, the pretty boy actor. "That tracks."

He grimaced. "But it wasn't there for me when I was injured, acting. Bruised? Swollen? Not able to walk? They wanted nothing to do with me."

It was hard to imagine a reality where no one would want Beau. "Do you ever think about going back to it?"

"I kind of apply it when I'm leading a class. But you know the reality of art—takes money to make it between gigs. I think I make more now than I would be acting, and I'm not exactly rolling in it."

I thought of the boxes of my failed business project that were reduced to one. Chris could only take so much of the stench of failure from me. "Kind of like how I'm an artist when I design a business card or a charity T-shirt. I'm not living the dream, but I'm living."

He kissed the top of my head; his fingers tingled my skin as he stroked my scalp. From this angle, he could probably see the silver streaks of my roots. When I first married Chris, this is what I thought marriage was going to be like—cherishing someone even as their cells broke down and sagged.

"Sir?"

"Hm?" My fingers still danced along the discolored part of his skin, where the scar was on his leg.

"Why did you say you were broken that night?"

A lump formed in my throat. I was glad he couldn't see my face. "Oh, you know, the mountain of failure that is my life."

"Art that didn't quite take off and a divorce?"

I nodded, but I realized the way he said it, he wasn't convinced.

I wasn't quite ready to connect the dots for him and explain that after the miscarriages had terrified Chris and me from sex, our weakened marriage crumbled when Claire offered him an escape route. She was someone successful, serious, and whole. "I feel like this conversation is sucking the sexy out of the room."

He directed me by my chin to tilt my head toward him. "Hm, I find learning more about you very sexy."

"You have an answer for everything." I closed the gap between us so our lips bristled together, featherlight.

And he kissed me on my nose. "Yep." The weight shifted in the bed. He was grabbing my e-reader off my nightstand. "Let's see what we have here." He pressed the button to open it. "*Submissive to the Moonman*. Dear Christ, I thought you were making up those titles."

I crawled over his lap to snatch my e-reader back, but he maneuvered it out of my grasp. He began reading it. *Klaxx whispered in my ear something I didn't understand, but the way he sent pulses to my cun—*

"This is absolutely filthy!" He looked at me with that smirk of his, which seemed to say, *naughty girl.*

He continued,

His silver-colored hand pushed me on the middle of my back, guiding me to the exam table to be probed in the most depraved way.

He set the e-reader on his lap. "Do you just read this or do you…" He waggled his eyebrows as his voice dropped off. His coy little way of asking if I masturbated to my alien erotica.

"I dot dot dot to it. Yes."

"With your fingers?" He drew my hands to his lips and kissed my fingers.

"Sometimes. Other times I count on—" I grunted as I reached over his lap to my nightstand drawer. Inside were Ole Reliable and Georgia the Destroyer of Clits, the new job title I gave my recently acquired gadget. "This and this. Accessories have a way of enhancing self-exploration." My toys rolled together in the sag of the mattress between us.

He picked up Ole Reliable and studied her. "You work this inside you?"

"Not all the time. I mostly like the vibrations."

"Where do you like to feel it?" The way he breathed that out had my complete attention.

I unbuttoned the top of my PJ shirt. "I like to feel it against my tits, along my stomach, thighs."

He handed me the e-reader. "Read your favorite part."

"Okay?" He propped my back up with enough pillows to place me in a comfortable recline. Perfect for reading with my elbows tucked to my side. He sat facing me, one of his long, sinewy legs hanging off the bed.

His fingers, longer than a human's, ghosted along the hem of the hospital gown, right where it tied in the back. I rested my cheek against the table. The metal cool—

As soon as I heard a *click*, the vibrator buzzed. Beau had turned it on.

I hugged the e-reader to my chest and scoffed. What was he brewing in that pretty little head of his?

"Keep reading," he said.

I licked my lips and scrolled back to the place I left off.

The metal cooled my cheek. I flickered my gaze up, meeting the lavender hue of his irises. His eyes were larger and possessed in them something more profound than I had ever seen in a human man. His anime gaze scanned my body, the galaxy-shimmer of it fixed to the ties of my gown.

Beau tugged at my top, unbuttoning each button, laying my boobs out for display. He dragged the silicone cock down the curve of my breast. My voice hiccoughed as I continued to make my way through the passage.

His slender fingers caressed from my cheek to my back and pulled the ties. At first—

I bucked off the bed. A vibrating sensation honed in on my nipple. What the—? Ole Reliable had grazed my tit. I swallowed and continued,

At first, he tenderly traced along the furrow of my spine. Why did it take an extraterrestrial to make me truly feel like a woman? His otherworldly strength ripped away the flimsy lace fabric of my panties.

My breath hitched as Beau smoothed the vibrator along my stomach, faint tremors traveled to my sweet center. He drew a line along the crease of my thigh, a light touch breezed my folds.

I read,

He rasped something once more that I did not understand, but he blinked slowly, reverently at my glistening, pink entrance. I'd like to think he was in awe of my body.

"Fuck!" I moaned.

Beau buzzed it across my clit. "It's getting good now."

Awe–awe of my b–body. Then his fingers probed my nether lips.

Beau lowered my shorts and freed them from my feet. Naked and spread out for him, I let him drag Ole Reliable around the other thigh.

One—one entered me. Softer and gentler than any human hand that had touched me. Klaxx's species didn't grow fingernails the way we did. His velvet smooth finger played around the ridge. When he added a second finger, I bit hard on my lip to prevent myself from—

My mouth dropped. I dug my heels into my comforter, kicking it into bunches. He glided the vibrator up and down my seam.

Prev–prev–prevent myself from fucking his beautiful fingers.

Beau teased the tip at my entrance.

Klaxx dug his fingers into my ass cheeks, spreading them apart. His loincloth dropped to the floor. "Please," I whined. "Please let me show you how we humans make love."

Ole Reliable disappeared inside of me, the base with the rabbit-ear-like tendrils tickled my clit. I shifted my hips to try to gain control, to keep the wild sensation from seizing my whole body. I was going to read like I was told to because I needed to hear him tell me what a good job I did—to call me "good girl." He'd push my body to the limit, and I'd still ask for more.

His ridged and pebbled cock penetrated me. I already felt so stretched around his much more ample member. "Not—not all of it." Klaxx grunted. With one more thrust, he was inside me to the hilt. I worked myself through the pinching pain.

"Beau, I'm going to come. I—"

He turned Ole Reliable off and tossed it to the side. "I want to feel it." He whipped his glasses off as if he was going to save the world.

I chucked that e-reader to the floor. We scrambled taking his shirt and shorts off with desperate tugs and ripping open a condom package. Sheathed in latex, he played around my sensitive vulva. He notched himself inside; I squeezed my legs around his ass. With one more thrust, he was inside.

"You feel amazing," he said breathlessly, stilling himself.

"How good have I been?"

"Such a good girl. My God, the way I feel you pulse around me." His pace picked up; his thrusts deepened. He cradled my head and held me so snugly. "The sexiest woman."

High-pitched sighs escaped his throat as he rocked faster and faster.

This time, I wasn't in a closet. I could unleash all the tension that had built up. I wailed. Sorry not sorry, neighbors.

"Too good. Too good, you're clenching me. Oh shit, I'm not going to last." He pumped into me, gripping my hips so hard, I'd have a bruise. The sounds he made as he climaxed made me so drunk. I could turn the rock star of cycle class into a puddle of a man.

We remained tangled together for some time, him still inside me. As the high wound down, I said, "Beau, you should—"

He rolled off me and lay back. Eyes closed, he slid the condom off and tied it, but he held it in his hand, sighing and grunting as if he needed to catch his breath.

Didn't exercise addicts like him have a bit more stamina? And at his age! "I wore you out." Honestly, I impressed myself.

"I'll recharge in no time." His chest moved up and down.

"You're absolutely winded." I laughed. At first, it was small, and then I shook. Tears rolled out of my eyes. "You need to do more cardio."

"In my defense, I never fucked to alien erotica, so color me pleasantly surprised." He then wrestled me to the bed to prove he had stamina.

After an additional round of orgasms, we ordered noodles and bao that were delivered to my door. In my kitchen, Beau showed off his dexterity with chopsticks. I bit into a morsel of bao, juicy with the perfect ratio of green onion to pork. Beau dangled a whole noodle above him, tilting his head back to slurp. He sucked it in, the noodle retracting into his mouth. A stray end clung to his lips.

"You're such a dork," I said. But of course, I was enraptured by how adorable he appeared, eating noodles like an utter trash panda.

Sexually satiated to a degree that didn't feel humanly possible and a belly full of good Chinese food, I dozed off in Beau's arms. I was his little spoon.

Chapter Fourteen

I awoke, feeling the weight in the bed shift. The outside was still dark when I heard Beau murmuring over his phone. "Yeah, I think I got what Starla got. Going around." He coughed. "Cancel classes? Yeah, I'll rest."

"What are you doing?" I whispered.

"I called in sick."

"Why?"

"So, I could spend more time with you."

"I'm leading you on a life of crime." I hit him with a pillow. "Lying that you're sick!"

"Calling in at work when you're not sick is not really a crime."

I fidgeted a bit, suddenly thankful that the morning's darkness obscured the features of my face. He didn't want to fuck and run. He *stayed*.

A complicated mix of emotions leaked out my eyes. I had a damn god in my bed, and I had him over and over again. How long had it been since I'd felt like this? Appreciated like a newlywed? I rubbed my face into my pillow to mop up the tears. Then I sniffled, unmistakably the sound of a good cry.

"Hey, hey, hey. What's up?"

I wiggled my way farther toward the edge of the bed, away from where the middle sank under our shared weight. "I'm going through some big feelings. No real cause. I think you got so far into my cervix, you hit a factory reset button, and my emotions are askew."

"You know what would fix it?"

"What?"

He curled behind me and held me tightly at my waist. "Hitting that button again."

"Pervert."

"Pervert's wench." He kissed the top of my head. "But you can talk to me about it."

I laughed, smearing the tears away. "I've read that book, *Pervert's Wench*. It has everything—true love, spanking, choking, deep throating, ass play, and of course a happily ever after."

He chortled and then suddenly became quiet. Rubbing my arm, he asked, "Are you making requests?"

I rolled my eyes, my disregard of kink invisible to him in the dark. My heart leaped at a damn joke where sex acts were the punchline.

I asked Chris for some of those acts early on. Spanking he took on with aplomb, but at the other things, he drew the line. He found them too demeaning and an utter kill to his libido. I assured him by my enthusiastic consent, an act wasn't demeaning. *You just want that because you're depressed,* he'd say. Not true but I wasn't going to force him into something he wasn't comfortable with. At the time, my "weirdo" curiosities weren't enough to implode my marriage. Little did I know it was the sign of the times. We couldn't be kinky, but we also couldn't be vanilla.

"Maybe?"

"I need you to say it." His erection poked my ass.

"Beau, I want you to spank me, hold me by the throat as you use me." Then came the real reasons that brought the tears. "I want to complicate that sunshine side of you. Let you have every part of me. Fuck my throat, my ass. Bring you to my dark side." I was turning myself on, saying everything I'd ever wanted in the bedroom. He moved his hips, creating the facsimile of sex. I reached up and touched the rough stubble on his jawline. "But maybe not all this weekend."

My fingers smoothed over the smile creasing his face. Perhaps this silly little affair had some room to grow. We could mess around until Beau got his senses together.

Beau shifted in the bed and handed me a condom. "Put it on me." He bracketed my head with his hands and hovered above me, his shadow lit by the glow of my alarm clock.

I stroked down his stomach, the lines of his hips I imagined in full light. I carefully rolled it on, going by the touch sensation rather than sight. With a few shimmies, I removed my shorts and guided his hand to my pussy.

"You're so ready for me," he whispered. Entering me in a strong, single thrust, his hips met mine. Once he found a rhythm, managing our bodies in the morning dark, he said, "Can I squeeze your throat?"

I nodded only before realizing my shadow didn't grant him enough permission. His care to do the right thing, even as the acts between us were kinky or taboo, was an entire squad waving green flags. "Yes. Squeeze my throat. I'll tap your hand if it's too much." I gave the top of his hand a slap. "Like this."

He forced his hips even deeper, groaning, and adjusted his weight as his right hand grasped my neck. On the outside, the picture would be considered intense, but the pressure was light enough not to inhibit blood flow or breathing—strong enough, though, to knock my sensations out of the stratosphere. As he picked up speed, I added my hand to the mix. I pulsed so violently that I practically shoved him out of me.

I tapped his hand to free my neck. He stopped and asked, "Are you okay?"

"Yeah, I just wanted to switch positions."

We adjusted to our sides, and he entered me from behind, his hand still on my neck. There, he could moan in my ear, bristle his cheek against mine. "You make me wild, Sir. Turn me into an utter caveman. You're the best."

His praise pushed me further over the edge. I was a whining lump of putty at this point. His hold of my neck tightened as he thrust powerfully into me. His sounds turned desperate, and he pumped and pumped until he was drained.

He flipped onto his back, the shadow of his chest heaved. The condom snapped as he pulled it off, and he chucked it in the direction of my trash can. He hummed and asked, breathless, "How was that for you?"

"Revelatory." I curled into his arms, finding that lovely spot to snuggle against his chest. "I recognized you were, um, o–ing as you said it, but am I really? Your best?"

"Certainly. Am I yours?"

Yes. Yes. A thousand times yes. Day one and we were already achieving a Master's in Sexual Chemistry. "You're no slouch."

Time lost all meaning for the rest of the weekend. We showered, slept, fucked. Not always in that order. He'd read from my absurd erotica, sometimes laughing hysterically, other times, tenting my high school shorts and fixing his gaze into that dark glower of his. As he danced around my kitchen making pancakes, which he launched two feet in the air to flip, I wondered how someone could be such a daisy one moment and thorn the next. I mean, he was singing Carly Rae Jepsen for chris-sake.

Chris believed the kinkier things I asked for in the bedroom were somehow a reflection of not only me but who he was in the outside world—people would see in his down vest layered over his Henley, "Hi, I'm Chris. I choke and spank my wife to make her come." That meant he was some tortured Christian Grey figure, a man with a dark past when he really was just a goober from Gorda Vista.

But Beau was such a damn people pleaser.

Sunday evening rolled around; Beau began his exit. Midwest style, in which it lasted for over an hour. He was back in his EverGreen & Fit cycling outfit that I had laundered and folded like his damn mom.

I asked, "What's the plan for tomorrow?"

"What do you mean?"

"Do I still workout at the gym? Is this purely physical or..." I wasn't quite ready to label us as boyfriend and girlfriend.

"Of course you should workout at the gym." He scratched at the stubble that grew in thickly over the course of the weekend. "What do you want this to be?"

I veiled my true wishes behind abject desire. I wouldn't mind Beau joining me in more Friday nights of delicious take out, PJs, and smut books. In that sense, he was the kind of friend I had been missing for a while. But I wasn't going to delve into that level of clinginess when my sheets were so freshly filthy from our activities. "We have a few goals I'd like to meet in the bedroom."

"And I'm prepared to help us reach that."

"Emotionally, however, I think we should go with the flow and not try to force anything." Good, I played it cool.

He adjusted his glasses. "Right."

I expected a stronger reaction from him. New relationship anxiety reared its ugly head. Of course, I *tried* to play it cool and then fumbled with an ever self-conscious, "What do you think?"

"I think you shouldn't do something you aren't comfortable with."

The needy part of me wanted him to tell me that my idea to "go with the flow" was the wisest, most perfect idea or the worst idea and he'd demand my heart or something swooningly romantic. I couldn't be honest with my feelings because honest feelings got stampeded on by life. I had sent us directly into a vague space between distance and intimacy because I was more comfortable being a chicken shit. "So do we have an understanding?"

He swayed his head from side to side. "Go with the flow. Makes sense." He pulled me by the band of my sweatpants. "Is it going with the flow if I say I better see you tomorrow?"

I shook my head and went for a kiss.

Chapter Fifteen

A t work, I stacked one more box of T-shirts for a family reunion in my arms. Lifting from my legs, I carried the boxes without a hitch to the customer's car. Once I unloaded the order into her trunk, I returned inside, whistling, and jumped across the counter rather than walk a few feet to open the gate.

"You're rather spry," Tina said, leaning in the doorway of her office.

I shrugged. Sometimes that gate was annoying and demanded a shortcut. Not to mention the customers loved it when I helped carry out their larger orders. Then it occurred to me why, and a giggle fit overtook me.

"What is it?" Tina had no clue about my weekend of being utterly worked out.

I cleared my throat. "I'm working out with my"—another round of giggles kicked in—"personal trainer."

"I can tell."

I pursed my lips together and fidgeted with a tendril of hair that had fallen out of my ponytail. How could she tell? Were my lips swollen from all the kissing? Hair frizzy from pillow friction despite my attempts at styling the lover's knots out? It was as if I was the teenage version of myself sneaking back into my house, mortified by what my mom recognized from my disheveled state.

"You're stronger."

I flexed my right bicep and gave it a poke. The muscle felt solid to the touch underneath my flannel shirt. "I am. Thank you for noticing." My hard work paid off, and I accomplished it with the help of Beau's knowledge, encouragement, and now affection. Warm fuzzies radiated from me, the side effect of freshly having my sex drive rocked over the weekend.

"Do you recommend your trainer?"

A cloud moved over me. Sharing Beau? Even though the idea was absurd, I wanted him to myself—to steal all the other hours he trained his clients and make the time with him mine. I shook the possessiveness from my head. "Yes, of course, I'd recommend him."

Tina laughed. "We'll be a couple of buff ladies."

Me? Buff? Maybe Tina needed her eyes checked, though I flexed my bicep again and admired the firmness. I never could imagine. I, Sir Hooper, was strong.

Though Tina provided the ego boost I needed at work, no amount of assurances had quieted my nerves when I entered the gym for our first post-wonder weekend training. I wiped the nervous sheen off my hand on my blobfish T-shirt. Scrawled under the fish slop, *I work well under pressure.*

I found him, past the turnstiles, leaning against the main desk in apparent uproarious conversation with Front Desk Frannie—er, Margie. She gave him a playful smack on his arm with the back of a clipboard. In mid smirk, he noticed me and straightened. "Excited for another sesh, Sir?" His expression seemed like the fake kind of joviality that riddled customer service.

I nodded and followed him to a studio room. This was going to be weird, wasn't it? We fucked, and now we'd do an awkward waiting game. Who would acknowledge that we'd seen each other naked first?

"I hope you're prepared to sweat." He held the door to the studio open for me.

I breezed by him, reliving the gravitational draw of his body. Fingers tracing over his muscles. Hands familiar with his warmth. I closed my eyes to possess him again, if only in my imagination. But it seemed the things I'd get down and dirty with today were a couple of mats, kettlebells, straps, and fitness steps.

"Today we'll work on your conditioning."

I narrowed my eyes to check if I wasn't missing a twinkle in his gaze or a slight turn in his mouth. Nothing.

I stood in front of one of the fitness steps and put my hands to my hips. "Bring it on, Coach."

I still got nothing out of him. He was all business, leading a warm-up of stretches. "Let's see how you do with the fitness step." His voice sent a shiver through me—the same steely tone when he told me to read a book before driving me into an orgasmic frenzy.

Up, up, down, down. Up, up, down, down. Prepared to sweat? This move was stinking easy, but he seemed unimpressed. "Lift your knees higher. The balls of your feet are hitting the edge, not the center of the step."

I completed another round and looked to him for approval.

"Faster."

I bit my lip and completed two more rounds, knees hitting the invisible line above my belly button, speed whipping through my muscles. Well?

"Five more."

I counted the "up, up, down, down" in my head.

"Out loud, Sir."

"Four, three..." I called the numbers loud over my panting.

"You miscounted. Do three more."

I scoffed. He couldn't be serious. The indifference in his face suggested otherwise. I sighed and started a round.

"Knees higher, again."

I did it again.

"I *said* count out loud."

"Three, two—"

"Faster."

As much as the cardio sent heat through me, I flared my nostrils as if I was a bull ready to charge. I shouted those numbers, lifted those knees, and pounded that plastic stair with the balls of my feet.

"Hm," he grunted dismissively, "seems like you're ready for the next set."

He modeled a dreadful thing that combined deadlifts and squats while swinging a kettlebell.

I completed one. *Tip from your hips*. Another. *Squeeze your glutes*. And again. *Deeper*. Got it. *Count to eight. Louder. You missed a rep. Add two more*. He did it again for the burpees and all the other exercises equivalent to the iron maiden.

By the end of the session, I took long, defiant pulls from my water bottle. I smeared eyeliner around my scowl with the hem of my T-shirt.

"You look like you want to say something to me, Sir."

"I didn't like that."

He chuckled. Not one of his charming ones. Mocking. "No one likes conditioning."

As always, a workout weakened me. What normally would be held in with a clench had been knocked loose with stretching and high-intensity interval training. "Not the conditioning. *You*."

He idly lifted the kettlebell in some all-too-easy bicep curl reps. "It's interesting how spite motivates you. You did four sets of thirteen. Most of my clients at this stage manage three sets of ten."

"Ah, the Zen of fuck you. Got it."

He stepped closer to me, the tip of his sneaker between mine. His dark gaze latched on to my searching one. Finally, I drew some emotion from him. "I'll do what I can to prove these limits you place on yourself are all in your head. I can stretch you, push you, and get you to embrace the discomfort," he scolded.

I slid my tongue over my lips and tasted the salt of my sweat off them while I rubbed them together. "You're still talking about personal training, right?"

"Take me to your car and find out."

The entire session had been a game. Torturing me had turned him on! "Now?" I asked.

His breath was as heavy as mine in one of his crucible-like HIIT sets. "Now."

I raised my chin, and a brat emerged. "But we must put our equipment away and spray down our workout area. Gym rules."

"Doesn't this good girl want to be bad?"

I barely used the time to shudder from his words before I sprinted out of the studio, Beau right behind me. My car was at the ass end of the parking lot, thanks to me wanting to get more steps in. But also, away from foot traffic and onlookers.

Without a verbal exchange, I unlocked the car. He entered the passenger seat and adjusted its electric motor settings, giving him as much room between the seat and the dash. I fumbled with the sun protector, which I usually only brought out in the summer. I blocked out the view of the front window. Gym goers having front row seats to whatever Beau had planned for me was a level of discomfort I wasn't quite into embracing yet.

Window blocked. Seat adjusted. Beau turned to me and said, "Well?"

I sprung over the center console. Our mouths met in a greedy kiss. As I moved my tongue against his, I positioned myself facing him on his lap. My hands gripped on to the top of the passenger seat.

He broke our kiss and sprinkled pecks across my cheek and down my neck. His stubble tickled, and I bit my lip to hold in a laugh. His lips softened along my pulse, and he flicked his tongue at the spot. "I thirst for your sweat."

I moved my hips, feeling him harden against me. "I could wring this shirt out right into your mouth."

He grunted in response, lifting my shirt and tugging at my sports bra. He lapped at my cleavage, a goblet of sweat.

I ached. I needed him. "Do you have a condom?"

He pushed me until my ass bumped against the dash. He fished a condom out of the pocket of his shorts.

"You're a Boy Scout," I said.

"I have to be prepared with you." He shimmied out of his shorts, his cock strained against the elastic. With one more yank, he freed himself. His cock bobbed and pointed to my car's roof; his shorts now bound him around his thighs.

I stared. I had spent all weekend operating my condo as a pants-free zone, but I still wasn't used to seeing the effect I had on him.

"Like what you see?" he rasped and fisted himself slowly, moving the skin of his uncut tip as he leaked down his shaft.

I bent down, straining in the awkward position, *embracing the discomfort.* I ran my flat tongue along the tip and then suckled on the end. I inhaled the ripe scent of him, savored the salty taste of him. His abs flexed, and he let out a sweet whimper.

My mouth let go of him, and I leaned back, rubbing my lips together. I ran my thumb across his tip and watched him twitch, watched his dark gaze weaken to warm and reverent. I licked his arousal off my thumb. "I thirst for you too."

He pulled at my shorts. Sweat and Lycra shorts weren't exactly copacetic with quickies in my compact, eco-friendly car. Ow! The band snapped back with a painful slap. We worked together, both giggling as I contorted out of those shorts. I was thankful I had stretched and completed hip openers at the start of my workout. I freed one leg while the tread of my shoe caught the other leg of my shorts. He slid the condom on and hugged my waist. In one fell swoop, his cock notched into my entrance.

The ache of longing became that pinch and throb of feeling full. I gasped.

"That face of yours is so pretty when you take my dick. The way your mouth parts. How your eyes get so big."

"Th-thank you," I breathed out. The response felt stupid the moment it left my lips. In turn, I moved my hips as much as the height of my car roof allowed and made sure not to squeeze my eyes shut, as much as closing them made it easier to adjust to his girth.

He caressed my face, his thumb lingering on my bottom lip. "I'm gonna fuck you, Sir. And spank you. And choke you. Will you tell me to stop if it's too much?"

I nodded.

"Louder."

"Yes."

"Now count. Count how much you pump my cock."

Jesus. I moved. Up, down. "One." And again. "Two." He guided me back so I was at the opposite angle of him. The new angle's depth ripped the breath from my lungs.

Before I could catch my breath—*Smack!* He spanked my ass. The shock and pain twisted inside me, building inside my core. I dug my teeth into my bottom lip as I let the wave pass.

"Count again."

"One." I moaned. As I worked, he placed my hands on my ankles. I was arched back, grinding and undulating. "Two." His thumb went straight for my clit. The sensation seized my entire body. I squealed.

Smack! "You missed your count."

I tried again. Another stinging slap against my ass. I failed once more yet each failure sent flutters from my womb. How was he going to send me over the edge? With his thumb at my clit, the hand at my ass, or his cock in my pussy? Thinking about it was enough to... enough to...

He lifted me off by my hips. The cold, hollow feeling without him cramped beneath my belly.

"You're not going to come until I tell you, you can."

"You're killing me, Beau."

His hands squeezed my throat. His lips grazed the shell of my ear. "Don't you want to be my good girl?"

I nodded. His latex-sheathed cock nudged along my slick cleft. I gave him one sloppy grind of my hips in assent.

"So impatient," he taunted. "You're gonna come riding my dick. But only when I tell you."

He slipped inside me with ease. His face mirrored mine as I bore down on him—the same parted lips and surprised eyes, I assumed. I counted to myself every circle of my hips as his grip at my throat sent a rush to my head. One, two, three, four. I shook. He hadn't told me I could come. I strained, grunted, fought. Tears trickled from my eyes. I couldn't handle it. I was reaching my limit. I had to tap out, must tap out. I must, I must, I must.

"Now be a good girl and come." He released his grip on my neck. I hugged him and the whole seat as I made some wonderful, guttural sound. His arms pinned me to him, and he groaned as he used his legs to thrust his hips deeper into me.

"I think people heard that across the parking lot." I kissed his temple. His sweat lingered on my lips. I loved the taste of his sweat.

He laughed as he eased out of me. "I can't believe we did that."

I blinked and gave my head a shake, chasing the auras in my vision. The dude had practically fucked me blind. "I think I need a moment." I rested my head on his shoulder.

He rubbed my back. His hand lowered to my ass and smoothed over the skin that had been turned into red prickles. "Take all the time you need." He kissed the top of my sweat-soaked head.

In reality, I needed about fifteen minutes. Most of that time putting on the shorts currently twisted around my ankle. But I wanted time to cease at this moment. I wanted to live on Beau's lap.

I had to be in subspace. Because this sweet, boneless feeling couldn't be anything else but subspace.

In my teens and twenties when I read articles about human sexuality to bask in the sordidness of it all, I learned women in their thirties had a surge in their sex drive, akin to a teenage boy's. After making it to my midthirties, I believed that those articles were full of shit. With age came more profound connections beyond the physical. But I found more and more that I lied to myself. Chris and I hadn't reached some sexual understanding better than a kid dictated by libido. We either lost ourselves in work or played house to such a degree that we didn't have energy for impulsive or even planned fuckfests. Add some miscarriages, and we may have been brother and sister by the end of our marriage.

The point was a sudden resurgence of sexual drive did not exist. A myth like unicorns and female ejaculation. *But, Sir, female ejaculation exists*, I'd hear from my naysayers. I didn't care what an academic article claimed. I wanted anecdotal proof!

And then came Beau.

We were ravenous.

He'd stay the night at my condo. When he learned I hadn't slept with anyone in my condo but him, he proposed christening each room with our sexual juices. Bedroom and bathroom were a given. The living room couch wasn't that difficult to check off either. On top of the kitchen counter was a welcome surprise as well as the floor of my office.

If that wasn't enough, he'd stop by the print shop. I'd announced to Tina that I needed to air out the back room from the smell of the freshly printed T-shirts. She didn't know I was getting pinned against the building in the alley, and I had to strategically wear skirts and stockings instead of pants. And I loved learning how his ass bubbled over the waistband of his shorts as we lowered it down just enough for easy access.

At the gym in a group class, I'd go through the motions and watch him drip and sweat everywhere while he led a class. Sometimes our gazes would meet in the mirror. He'd answer with a small smile, and I'd bite my lip. During a personal training session, he'd shamelessly offer to help me stretch, pulling my leg back to get deeper into my hamstring, when I knew from the wicked glow in his eyes he wanted to try the exact maneuver in bed. The touches he'd give to "improve my form" lingered longer.

After another spontaneous rendezvous in my economy car, I fell out of it laughing. His fans, the front row cycle divas with matching bra and short sets and impossibly white tennis shoes, walked by. They were also proponents of getting more steps in and stared as Beau and I giggled at my clumsiness. He swatted me on the ass, and I swear one of the front row cycle divas scowled. Maybe we could work on being discreet.

Chapter Sixteen

I skipped out of Clarissa's styling chair with fresh roots when I received a phone call from Fiona. In this week's call I regretted picking up, Fiona monologued about Mom trying to poison everyone at family dinner with salad dressing that had been in the refrigerator for well over a decade.

I droned, "Oh yeah? Uh–huh."

"How are things with you?" she asked.

"That's wild." I caught myself on autopilot. "Oh, uh, great actually."

"Great? Really?" Fiona never believed me when I shared good news.

"Working on my physical fitness, starting to draw again." I wasn't sure if Beau was sister newsworthy.

"Wow. What are you doing?"

A man in his twenties. "Cycling, strength training, Pilates. A little bit of everything really."

"You sound really happy."

"You can hear it in my voice?"

"Yeah. I can't point out any specifics."

It was less than half an hour to the start of cycle class, and I needed to change, get a good seat, and properly warm up. "Huh, well, I have to cut this short. I'm off to a cycle class."

Imagine my surprise when after a couple weeks of my life revolving around Beau and his dick, I arrived to class to discover Starla filling in for him. I checked my phone for any missed phone calls or texts. I didn't exactly give Starla my all during the cycle class, as I kept looking at my phone, expecting *something* from Beau. Maybe Starla knew something? After the disappointing class, I waded through the Starla fan club to ask her where Beau was.

"He said it was an emergency. Something with his mom and dad."

He never talked about his mom or dad. Jealousy swirled with bile in the pit of my stomach. Starla knew more personal details about him than I did, and I knew what his balls looked like.

I sent a text and then a call that went straight to his messages. In this abyss of incommunicado despair, I did something I wasn't proud of. I drove to the street he had gestured to on our walk back from Vine and Spirits.

I slowed my car to a crawl to find the house with the basketball hoop in the driveway. At the top of the cul-de-sac, I found a house that fit the description, a sand-colored ranch home with white shutters and trim. The front yard appeared curated with curved, pebbled pathways and flourishing drought-resistant plants. The home was gorgeous in its simplicity.

I parked alongside the street and took a deep breath before leaving my car. This was an invasion. If this was his home, he hadn't invited me. I was sort of stalking and forcing my way in.

I knocked on the door and counted backwards from one hundred. If nobody answered by then, I'd take that as a sign and drive back home like a normal person. In the final ten seconds, I shifted my weight to pivot around.

Then a slender older woman answered the door who appeared straight out of a prescription drug ad with a head of thick, white hair to her chin, and hazel eyes that were otherworldly. Beau had mentioned his roommate was older. I didn't know what that meant, but this woman seemed old enough to be his mother.

"Hello," I said, "is Beau here?"

"He's watching television with his father. Beau! Someone's here to see you."

He entered the foyer, and his eyes bugged. "Sir."

"I know, I know, but Starla said you had an emergency come up, and I worried. And now I'm here, waving red flags everywhere."

He shoved his hands into the pockets of his gray sweatpants. "My dad fell off the ladder earlier today. I took him to the emergency room."

"I'm so sorry. Is there anything I can do to help?"

He craned his neck and looked off to the room on the other side of the foyer. He looked like he was about to throw up.

I fucked up. I shouldn't be there. I seriously pole vaulted over a bunch of boundaries.

Sunshine and rainbows Beau lowered his head as if ashamed. He murmured, "I live with my parents."

"Oh." I totally did that movement with my head where I shifted it back as I considered what he said. I shook the expression off because I was making a judgy face, and I so didn't want to be making a judgy face. He wasn't ashamed of me but worried how I would react, knowing a full-grown man's roommates were his parents. "Do you think I care about that?"

I used the moment to ask myself if I did. Growing up, even with the worst economy since the Great Depression, elder millennials like me put value in living on our own. We had shitty apartments where we'd invite friends over and pre-party before hobbling to the club in stilt-like heels and peplum tops. In my nice but not show-stopping condo, I'd probably kind of love dividing the rent with my mother. I'd have half the sanity but also half the cost.

And we really lived in one of the most expensive places *in the world*. Everyone wanted the Gorda Vista feel with the promise of escaping to the cities sandwiching us. But no one ever wanted to go to those cities. They loved beautiful, over-priced Gorda Vista.

I stepped forward. "I don't care about that."

Relief smoothed the crease in his brows.

"But I want you to feel comfortable telling me these things because..." Because this take-it-as-we-go arrangement was taking me straight to relationship town despite better judgment. Although some johns really cared about the prostitutes they hired. Not that I hired Beau for bedroom activities. Though the relationship had an odd transactional element to it. "I care about you."

His eyes went full-on puppy. "They still make me do chores, you know. I was supposed to clean the gutters, but I've been a little distracted lately. Dad took it upon himself to climb up there."

I swallowed. I was the distraction. A sick feeling overcame me. "Do you feel guilty about what we do?"

"No, but I should be spending more time at home."

I didn't expect to be this disappointed in slowing things down. Jesus, I needed to chill and just go back to being a lonely lady who masturbated after reading smut. "I shouldn't be here. I invaded. I'll see you when I see you."

I was about ready to head out the door when he added, "If the shoe was on the other foot, I'd want to be there for you too."

I shimmered internally. "I could help you." At thirty-seven years old, I was still letting a dick make me do stupid things. "With cleaning the gutters."

His lips twitched, as if he was fighting a smile. "You want to do that? With me?"

No, I didn't want to clean out the gutters. Ick. Gross. I seriously hired people for that shit. It was one of the few benefits of having my ex-husband as a landlord. But spending time with Beau and helping him care for his family? I wanted to do that.

"I was going to get started with it tomorrow, after boot camp and core class."

I had a plan for my Saturday. "I'll be right over."

He stared at me for the longest time. "Should we hug or something?"

I stepped farther into the foyer, and we embraced. He smelled so clean, like those air fresheners labeled *Aloe Winds* or *Connecticut Clouds*—as if he had the world's best laundry detergent. Hugging in his parents' house somehow felt more intimate than exchanging bodily fluids. I adjusted my head and looked up at him. He lowered his lips to mine, and we pecked.

"See you tomorrow."

"Tomorrow."

Chapter Seventeen

I showed up wearing my overalls and long-sleeved T-shirt with the sweetest looking bunny on it. It was a special print because it felt fuzzy to the touch. The statement? *Cute but Useless.* Beau had a good laugh at it, particularly as I flapped around trying to get the gutter sludge off my shirt sleeve.

The gutters were absolutely disgusting. They were full of the brown sludge made from rainwater, brown leaves, and birdies' little attempts at nests. A twee bit of revenge burst from me, and I threw a wad of gutter goodness in his direction.

He responded by chasing me around the yard as if we were kids playing tag. The training was paying off. I didn't stand much of a chance against Beau, but I kept up. That is until he stuffed some leaves down the back of my shirt. I wiggled and fished some leaf–twig–bird–nest combo out of my bra right as his parents came out to oversee our progress.

I had to be making the best impression wiping gutter sludge off myself.

"This is Sir," Beau said as he introduced me to them. His parents handed us some glasses of lemonade as a reward for his hard work.

"As in knight," his mother said.

"She's my um... my um..." Beau stammered over the title he'd now bestow to me. "A friend of mine."

I'd like to say it was no big deal. After all, I told him last weekend, "Go with the flow." but it stung. Obviously, my reaction was of someone whose last sexual encounter was with the person she married. I had all sorts of cognitive behavior therapy to unfuck that part of my brain.

"How'd you two meet?"

"The gym," I replied. Beau's ears turned red.

"You're an instructor?"

"No, an instructee," I answered.

Beau fumbled over his next few words. I'm sure he was trying to come up with an explanation that sounded a bit better than admitting he hooked up with his client. "She walked into the gym, and we sort of hit it off. Do you see her T-shirt? She designs those."

Beau's mom squinted her eyes as she read the message. "Cute but useless. How... how *interesting*." Can't blame her for underreacting to my niche humor. That was why the whole ItsyBizzy store failed.

His dad, the perfect match to Beau's elegant, straight-out-of-a-drug-commercial mom, shook a finger, the one on his cast-free arm. His much-the-same puppy-dog eyes glowed with excitement. "Is this the one you said, 'made you laugh' a while back?"

Beau mentioned me? A while back? I was *squee*-ing on the inside. He, on the other hand, blushed until he matched the red of his ears as he nodded his head.

"How's your wrist, Dad?" Beau opted for the change in conversation.

His dad lifted his cast–covered arm. "Eh." He stretched out in the lawn chair. "Beau never brings anyone around."

His dad wasn't reading the total bashful expression taking Beau over. I said, "I kind of insisted on helping him. When he wasn't at the gym, I took it upon myself to check up on him."

"Good that he has someone worrying about him. Right, Beau?"

Beau nodded but squinted at the sun, not quite the enthusiasm of leading a workout. His embarrassment that I sensed left him tongue–tied.

Beau and I behaved as the Bishops watched us from their back patio. His dad barked orders, especially at Beau.

Before the late afternoon, we had those gutters sparkling and the organic bins full. We had to end our time together because he needed his family night, and the Bishops were definitely not my family. My family would tell us we organized the leaves and twigs incorrectly before I'd feel back in the cold embrace of my Midwest home. But something wistful came up as I hugged him and set out to go back to my empty condo.

So, I smeared some yard waste on his cheek just so he knew that, although I may be more than a decade older and physically at a disadvantage, he should be on his toes waiting for me.

Chapter Eighteen

I prepared for my weekend evening ritual: a bath with my bath bomb, a cup of tea, and slugging so many products on my face that I'd age in reverse like Benjamin Button. I put on my fluffy, terry cloth bathrobe and prepared to give my gutter-cleaning, tired muscles a soak.

I heard a gentle knock. The doorbell camera confirmed Beau was on my doorstep.

"Two for two in answering the door in a state of undress." He embraced me, grabbing my ass and going in for a kiss.

I split us apart for a moment. "I thought you wanted some family time."

"I'm sure we can negotiate a housework/sex life balance."

We soaked in my bathtub, his back against my boobs and my legs hugged around him. I stroked his wet hair. His expression was contemplative and not quite its purely sunny self. "Thank you for helping me today," he said.

"Strangely, I liked cleaning gutters with you."

"I needed you there. At the hospital." He interlaced his fingers with mine and sighed. "I hated being there with him. I was getting these body tremors as if I was back after the accident."

"I wish I could've been there for you." I hooked my chin on his shoulder. "You know you can count on me, right?" I wasn't going with the flow. I was flowing and going straight to relationship labels and coupledom. Maybe we should name our situation "friends with benefits." Friends cleaned gutters and were there for each other in emergencies. I'd love to have a friend like that.

He walked his fingers on the ledge of the bathtub seeming distracted. "Do you think I'm a loser?"

Nothing could be further from the truth. I had my legs wrapped around the hottest guy in town.

I laughed. "Has that been bothering you this whole time?"

"Living with your parents because you can't afford to live anywhere else isn't exactly sexy."

"Well, you're already handsome, funny, and great in bed. If you added living in a mansion you own, I think I'd have to slash your tires to balance out your karma. You just can't be that perfect." I ran my fingers along the ridges of his torso. "Besides, I like you. Every part." I painted his body with suds, thinking how I had captured his dimensions in a silly cartoon. My electronic sketch pad had accumulated an embarrassing amount of Beau prototypes, as if he were a muse.

Fresh out of the bath, I lay on my stomach as he helped me apply my eczema association approved moisturizer. I learned how much he loved my legs and ass with how many strokes they received.

He said, "Your hamstrings are tight. You need to stretch them out better. I know someone who offers stretch classes."

"Is that someone you?" I nuzzled my cheek against the arm propping my head. His thumbs grazed high enough to touch my pussy.

I arched toward his playful fingers. "Are you initiating?"

"You initiated the moment you opened the door in that robe of yours."

"Then you should see me on Sundays. I practically live in the thing."

His hands stayed high and spread my wetness. "Turn over."

I complied. He dragged me across the bed until my head hung off the ledge.

"What are you up to?" I asked. My pussy throbbed at all the possibilities.

He stood over me, his penis bobbing inches from my chin. "Lick."

I opened my mouth, held out my tongue, and traced it along his shaft, prodding the sensitive area right under his dusky head. He sucked in a breath between his teeth and responded in kind by pinching my nipples, which sent lightning bolts south. I writhed and wriggled. But his hands smoothed down my torso and braced my legs. Once I stilled, he didn't help my erotic tumult when his fingers dipped and stroked along my seam.

I hummed against his tip and popped it in my mouth. The sounds he made sent as much of a surge between my legs as his fingers did, spreading and caressing. I wasn't sure who started it, but I took more of him into my mouth. I breathed deeply through my nose, opened my mouth *ah*, and spread my tongue. He thrust his hips, his cock going down my throat. For a moment, I resisted, gagging on him, yet he held himself deep. I relaxed again, taking sips of air through my nose, and he resumed fucking my throat. After a few pumps, he pulled out. I inhaled the fresh and crisp air. I used my slobber to give him sloppy wet strokes.

"Again?" he asked, his voice growly and needy.

"Sure." Could I sound more Midwestern? Maybe if I said, "You make my pussy go *ope*."

"Beg for it."

I had to twist my nipples just to contain myself. I loved it when he got bossy. "Please, please, I need you to fuck my throat."

He shoved himself past my lips, not as nicely as before. The force sent more vibrations all over my body. His fingers plunged inside me, hooking and rubbing against my G–spot as fast and desperate as his thrusts. And then, I learned, female ejaculation wasn't so mythical while coming hard, my cries muffled by his cock.

"You're so good at throating my dick. I have to stop before I lose control." My body was still shaking when he threw me around the bed like a rag doll, finally resting my head against the pillows. He lowered himself between my legs. "I'm going to show you what a good girl you've been."

"Show me with that mouth and tongue," I pleaded.

Oh, and he did. Even rubbed his nose in it like he lived off it, as if he needed me like oxygen and water. I knew multiple orgasms existed. They weren't a common feature in my bedroom games. But I had to suffocate him with my thighs as another torrent ripped right through me. He pulled me up to his face and kissed me, making sure his tongue shared my taste. A drug never got me this high. I didn't know my name, what day it was. I was just a body that needed Beau servicing it. He flipped me onto my stomach and pulled my hips up so I could present myself to him. I rested on my forearms as he gently caressed my ass cheeks. Then he gave it a sharp slap. I was screaming, laughing, crying in outer space.

"Again." I moaned. He landed another slap on the other ass cheek. I bit down on a ripple in my sheets. He probed me, slicking my juices over my pleated entrance. "I can't wait for you to fuck me there." I whined because I'd been reduced to a begging mouth and body.

"Patience." He hissed. Foil ripped, and he sheathed himself in a condom. He teased my pussy with the tip, dragging it from my willing hole to my clit.

I wiggled my hips. "I need it."

He gave me just a bit, so I showed off how much his core classes strengthened my intimate muscles. He pulled out, his thumb rubbing my aperture. My hips searched for him, and my soaking wet entrance sheathed him until his hips met my ass. He gripped my cheeks and pumped slowly. I moved against him to show how rough and fast I needed it. I was mindless.

His fingers dug in my hips, and he went wild.

He used me and used me until he came. He gave me another playful slap on my ass as he settled.

I stretched out, lying prone and utterly obliterated. "I'm floating."

I heard him move around my bedroom, the snap of latex as he ditched the condom, the glide of the sheets as he slid behind me in bed. He drew me in close to his chest, and his fingers skirted over my back. Listening to the rumble of his voice through his chest brought me back to Earth. "I'm needing a thesaurus to find the right adjectives to say. That was... a personal best?"

"You didn't just use a workout term."

"I did. If I knew cleaning gutters was going to turn me on so much, I'd have done it sooner."

"Now we have to ask your parents if they want anything raked, weeded."

He laughed. A beat passed that somehow caused the tension to grow.

"I feel like you're about to say something," I said into his chest.

"Do you want to get some dinner and drinks?"

I tilted my chin so I looked up at him. "Now?"

He nodded. I was too sex drunk to object. This wasn't what personal trainers with benefits did. This was something couples did.

"Holy moly, we'll have to shower again. I can't wait to see my water bill this month," I said.

"Actually, I want to get all dapper for you. Back here in half an hour?"

Before I had feeling back in my legs, he left my apartment in a sunny burst.

Chapter Nineteen

I was going out to dinner! On a weekend! In the evening! It was in times such as this one that I relied on the back of my closet, which contained those bits and pieces I'd collected over the years and never had the bravery to wear out. Or, the dresses I wore once to a special event, and nothing special ever happened again. I chose a navy, body-hugging cocktail dress with mesh sleeves and back. The only way I could wear it was with one of those bizarre bras without a back and a giant plunge in the front. I curled my hair, put on my makeup. I even glued on some eyelashes! By the time I tottered in my platform heels, the best type of heels by the way because I get support and length, Beau was at my door looking gorgeous in a gray suit, no tie, and a plain white collared shirt.

"You look beautiful," he said. He took the very words out of my mouth.

"Thanks. Same to you, though. But you look amazing even covered in gutter dirt."

He spun me around to check me out. No one had ever spun me around to check me out. "You do too."

We walked to L'Hommes aux Pommes, one of the fanciest restaurants in Gorda Vista. It had been used for filming a few movies, even. That's how large and fancy it was. We didn't have reservations but found a stoop to drink and eat at the bar.

For once, we were on even turf. I turned as many heads in my age bracket and above as Beau did. I considered tonight the only night I could be the Barbie to his Ken.

"Sir, is that you?" a familiar voice called out to me. I turned to find Chris and Claire. Chris, looking like a dad about ready to board a boat, and Claire in some kind of floor-length frock that screamed "Under His Eye." Still quite pregnant.

"Chris! Claire! Imagine seeing you here." I chuckled nervously as I swiveled completely around on the stool. Beau turned around too and put his hand on my lower back.

"Trying to squeeze in as many date nights before—" Claire rubbed her growing belly.

"I thought I made a reservation, but I failed to hit the confirmation button. Now here we are at the bar, next to you." Chris's shoulders tensed up, which meant he wanted to crawl away and hide. And me? Wanted to point a neon sign to the hand at the small of my back.

"Chris, this is Beau, my... my..."

"Date," Beau answered. He shook Chris's hand. Beau was all neutral calm, being the alpha in this situation.

"Chris is my—"

"Ex." Chris finally broke the handshake. He had a stern crook to his eyebrows as if *he* was sizing *Beau* up. As if the dude still had some kind of say with what I did with my life. "Claire and I were thinking about leaving anyway. A pregnant woman at a bar doesn't look good to outsiders."

Claire whispered loudly in Chris's ear, "I was craving their braised escargot."

I gestured to the empty seats at the end of the bar, far from us and allowing only a limited amount of awkward eye contact. "It's really not a big deal if you sit at the bar. Water under the bridge and all."

Claire whispered something in Chris's ear. When she was done, she announced, "Great!" and waddled her way to the seats and claimed the place with her coat, scarf, and oversized purse—perfect for eventually being full of diapers.

Beau nudged me with his knee. He leaned in, moved my hair to the side, and whispered in my ear. "Do you need some time with him?"

I shrugged. Most of my interactions with Chris during and post–divorce involved being in transition. Determining which of our former home's junk went with me and the condo, packing it in boxes, and helping me unpack. Furtive glances and heavy goodbyes suggested there was so much more to talk about, but we let it slide. That was what happens when a marriage ends with indifference.

"I know the maître d' and he said he might be able to wedge us in at a table. I'm going to check how that's going." Beau stood up and buttoned his blazer. With his hair, he was a shade taller than Chris, which surely shrunk my ex's balls a bit.

"Honest minute?" Chris asked. He leaned across the stool that Beau had once been sitting in.

I swiveled my legs toward the bar. They only pointed to Beau like a divining rod. "Go for it."

"How'd you two meet?"

"He's my personal trainer." Even though our sessions were benefiting him as much as me. "Maybe was? Not sure."

Chris raised his mouth into a simpering smile. The yacht-less captain relished that Beau was a few notches down on the ladder of money and success, the true alpha currency in Gorda Vista. "How old is he?"

"Almost thirty."

He chortled. "In a few years?"

"Maybe."

"Got to hand it to you, did not see that on the Sir Garfield BINGO card." He adjusted the cufflinks on his shirt. "Are you two serious?"

"I go by Hooper again." I narrowed my eyes. "Since when did you care about my love life?"

"I don't really care. Just making conversation." He laughed, sardonically. The kind of one he did quite often near the end. His gaze floated over me, foot to head. "Did you own that dress when we were together?"

"Yup. Wore it to your company fundraiser." I tossed my hair back, enjoying the appearance of youth. Thank you, Clarissa.

"I'm sorry I forgot." He flashed a smile. The slight snaggle of his incisor had disappeared thanks to some straightening. To believe I had once loved that crooked grin, which was now indistinguishable from an *After* photo in a brochure.

I was so flipping glad he was in the past, regardless of how serious and how much he was by my side during some shit times. But with how intense and attentive Beau was in the last two months, had Chris ever been that present in our eleven years of marriage? "I'm not."

On cue, Beau marched back from wherever he disappeared to.

"Nice seeing you, Sir. I have to admit, you clean up well." Chris joined Claire at the end of the bar.

I swiveled again to face Beau and tugged him by the lapels of his jacket. He smirked. "Are they looking at us? Should I shove my tongue in your mouth?"

"Maybe some light PDA."

He placed both his hands on either side of my face. I warmed with how secure this made me feel. He kissed along my jawbone, on the side of my mouth, and finally planted a suckling kiss on my lips. "You really look gorgeous."

We ate and drank enough to feel lightheaded. The bill arrived. Being L'Homme aux Pommes, it was more than a little steep. "I got this," I offered.

He put his hand on top of the vinyl folder bearing the receipt. "But I was the one to invite you."

I grabbed the other end of the bill. "Then we can split it fifty-fifty," I said.

He jerked it away. "Seriously, I can take care of it."

"It's alright. You don't have to impress me. We both know—"

"That I live with my fucking parents."

The bite of his voice stopped me dead in my tracks. I was stupidly going to say I was better off financially. I was the purchaser of an unnecessary amount of training sessions, and he didn't let our affair stop me from prepaying at the beginning of each week.

Though I was being laissez-faire about paying a fancy restaurant bill, my eventual financial crash loomed over me too. Tina was probably, most definitely going to cut my hours. In a few more years, I'd be out of alimony payments. Eventually, I'd need to move out of my condo so I no longer had an ex-husband/landlord. And with how I noticed Chris sending a glare from up the bar, it would be sooner rather than later.

I let go of the bill and let him pay. "But I'm getting it next time."

We walked back to my home in silence after dinner. I wasn't sure how soon our next evening out was going to be.

Chapter Twenty

Despite my rising worries, Tina hadn't made good on her threat at work. But because of the looming cutbacks, I behaved myself better while on the clock. No more back alley rendezvouses with Beau over the lunch hour.

Tina did, however, cut corners. We usually had a sharpener come for the paper cutter every few months. Tina was trying to double the time, and we were paying for it. I had to reprint and cut a batch of business cards as the cutter gave them a cute little curve. It wasn't noticeable staring at an individual card, but as a giant stack of business cards inclined up the storage box, yeah, it was pretty obvious. Orders were going to take longer to fulfill since I could only use half the paper cutter, the half that didn't fuck up orders.

Despite the after-dinner, bill-paying hiccough, Beau and I quickly became domesticated. Instead of coming over to mine for *just* sex, we added things like cooking dinner together three times a week. What would normally be leftovers for my lunch became Beau's serving, and I enjoyed how my condo wasn't quiet anymore. But we didn't talk about the restaurant bill snafu.

I decided to handle the bill blowback by having my actions speak louder than words. The next weekend, I offered to join him and his parents for dinner but only after we completed Beau's chores. Further, on my lunch breaks from The Mighty Pen, I'd go walk another sandwich to Beau at the gym. It was so wholesome being the woman who brought him his lunch. Onlookers would have no idea that he made me come from slapping my ass or my titties.

We had finished one of our parking lot quickies. He adjusted the waistband of his green gym shorts as I straightened my new corduroy skirt I picked up at the thrift store near the gym. In addition to wearing skirts to make the parking lot quickies quicker, I also had to keep buying more of them, so I wasn't always washing the same three skirts that I owned.

Beau ran his fingers through his hair so it could achieve its telltale voluminous curve. "We should probably stop doing this at the gym."

I was surprised how much the disappointment stung. I liked how a fresh round of sex added a youthful blush to my skin. "Oh yeah? Margie catching on?" I buttoned my mouth to one side to stop an oncoming frown. I wouldn't want to explain to Beau that I liked this more than just the orgasms. I liked spending an unhealthy amount of time with him. To hide my reaction, I reapplied makeup in my compact. "The fogged over windows are clueing her in? Or was it the time you touched my taint when you corrected my downward dog?"

His crooked smile creased his handsome face. "No, it's... How do I put this?" He sighed and scratched at the back of his neck. "I've applied to audition for the EverGreen & Fit app."

"What does that mean?"

"I'd have to go to the San Francisco studios and audition."

"Yeah, but what does it mean about your stint here?"

"If I got offered a spot on the app, I wouldn't be here anymore. I'd be possibly commuting. The pay is enough that I may consider a new living situation, my own place in the city."

I needed a word to describe enjoying that he was always a few blocks away from me for lunch and sex. If he was all the way in San Francisco, he could no longer be my personal trainer. Without that aspect of the relationship drawing us together, it might not be so likely he'd still come by late in the evening after a long commute. But *he* might be more professionally fulfilled, and that mattered more than any of my complicated feelings, adding way too much weight to this news. "Wow, you've really thought about this."

"But I need you to help me be on my best behavior." He wagged his finger at me. I grabbed it and bit the tip. "And you're already failing."

"So corporate is keeping a watchful eye." My stomach lurched at the next idea. Play time might be over even before a possible move to the city.

He checked his reflection in the rearview mirror and nibbled on his bottom lip. "I was wondering if you'd help me after classes to work on my audition. Music, banter, solid fake woos to real woo ratio."

I had warned him that appealing to my weirdo demographic would be a black hole to bottom lines. "You think I'd be good for that kind of feedback?"

"I wouldn't be here if it weren't for you."

Damn, he was turning me into a blushing emoji.

"I have to warn you," he said, "Helping me with my audition would probably happen at night after evening classes are finished."

"And then we'd debrief at my place."

"Very much so." He held my chin and kissed me.

Chapter Twenty-One

S mack in the middle of having to be at our best behavior, Beau brought a present with him during one of our dance-in-the-kitchen-and-make-dinner nights. I opened a velvet-lined box containing three metal spade-shaped *things*. Each was a different size. The stem ended with a heart-shaped jewel.

The familiar shape of the object finally dawned on me. "Did you buy me a set of butt plugs?"

Beau nodded with a crooked smirk.

"That's the most romantic gift I've ever received."

He grabbed me by the center of my T-shirt that had a blurry raccoon surrounded by multi-colored auras. The title, *Disassociating Like a Girlboss.*

"Let's work up an appetite."

He fished through my nightstand, knowing where I kept my lube. He took my shirt off, shifted me around and pulled my pants off. I stepped out of them, giving them a kick across my bedroom floor. He gave my back a shove so my hands braced against my bed. Biting into my shoulder, he unhooked my bra and let it drift down my arms.

I attempted to turn around to help him at least achieve the same level of nakedness I was at. He gripped my bicep, strong enough to leave finger-shaped bruises. "Stay still," he ordered through clenched teeth.

I responded with a nervous chuckle. "Okay."

"Give me your hands."

I reached behind, and he crossed my arms at the middle of my back. I turned my head to the side.

"Look at me."

I opened my eyes. The warm, puppy-dog brown eyes were dark and cutting behind his horn-rimmed glasses. Seriously, I didn't think they had a Cycle Daddy vibe on the EverGreen & Fit app. That might nail his audition.

His fingers skirted down the groove of my spine. They hooked into the band of my underwear, which he guided down my legs. He kneeled, staring right into that pink place of need I had for him. His knuckles grazed along my folds. "Good girl. You stay wet for me."

I smiled proudly, watching his mouth disappear over the slope of my ass. He tongued my wet channel, and I leaned into his face wanting to feel myself fucked on every part of him.

"Still." He smacked my ass.

The amount of will it took to stop twisting—I dug my teeth into my comforter.

Purposely avoiding my unfucked rosette, he guided his tongue to my clit, burying his nose in me. My legs shook as I verged on losing control.

"I live for the way you taste."

He spread my cheeks and feasted. It didn't take much to get me wailing for the neighbors to hear. Sorry society, if they insisted on shoving us into properties with shared walls, those walls are going to shake with the way Beau surprised my body and worked me over. They had to be used to it by now.

His attention moved from my pussy to my ass. He tongued and licked my pleated entrance. The weight of him moved off me. I heard the squirt of lube and sensed his hand finding the spot he had warmed up so well with his mouth. Then—I jumped. Goddess on high, that was cold! He caressed my aperture slowly, the lube warming to my body. A pinch, then his finger was knuckle deep in my ass.

"How does this feel?"

I breathed, high and girlish. "Good?"

"That's not the enthusiasm I was expecting." He took his finger away.

"Jesus, Beau, you feel so fucking good. Don't you dare stop."

He directed my body from bent to standing. His hand held me by my throat as he kissed the soft spot behind my ear. "I need you to be that sure at all times. No half-assed, kinda, sorta. Got it?" His words had me panting. His mouth met the side of mine, giving me sloppy, hungry kisses that tasted of me.

I closed my eyes and listened to him pump more lube.

"I didn't say close your eyes."

I opened them. In front of me, he held up the smallest butt plug. He huffed on it, warming it with his breath. I rubbed my lips together to keep myself from drooling because, dear God, he was sexy.

Another shove, I was back to bent over my bed. A slight invasion of metal pressed against me. He teased and teased, pushing the plug and circling it. I opened for him, and it slipped in with ease, no pain—just the pleasure of being worked tenderly. "How's that?" he asked.

I laughed, a nervous flutter of energy possessed me. "That's it?"

"Don't overdo it." He flipped me over and laid me across the bed. On my back, the plug prodded more vividly. The pressure from my behind built up a different kind of pleasure around the front of my pelvis. He pulled at the collar of his T-shirt, lifting it off. His torso's sculpted perfection was always a visual treat for me. I couldn't help but reach out and run my hands over him. There was something so smug about his smile. The fact that he knew he exuded such ideal sexiness compounded my lust for him. He held up Ole Reliable—his way of announcing what was next in my multi-course meal of my fantasy.

He kissed the tip of my vibrator. I squirmed at the idea of breaking all taboos, having my dick sucked, using my cock to fuck him so we broke every boundary of man and woman and knew our souls would find a way to eke every ounce of pleasure out of each other.

His eyes lit up. "You like that?"

I pulled and pinched my nipples to stoke the fire. "Yes." I panted out, "Suck my dick."

He licked along the side of it.

"I said *suck*."

He kneeled over me between my legs and grasped my throat. "Are you watching?"

Between his bossiness and the plug making its presence quite known, I had to take deep breaths to stop another orgasm bursting from me. His gaze fastened to mine, peering above his glasses made askew from our activities. He opened his mouth and took about three inches in, hollowing his cheeks. He laughed and said, "This is a lot harder than it looks."

"Don't worry, we can set small goals for improvement."

He didn't let my punchline last for long. He turned it on, buzzed it against my swollen bud. My body jerked. As I calmed to the sensation, he glided the tip down my folds and teased around my channel. Bit by bit, he guided it inside. "How does that feel?"

I was full from both sides. The vibrations of Ole Reliable bounced off the plug, sending tremors everywhere below my waist. A few more plunges of my vibrator, and I was moving my hips wildly—so close to bursting my eyes were rolling in the back of my head.

Then nothing.

The buzzing sound stopped with a click. I smoothed my hands over my body to finish what he started because if I didn't I would die.

He grabbed my wrists and lifted them above my head. "Keep your hands off or I'll tie you up."

"Promise?"

He backed off me and searched around my room, zeroing on my fluffy robe draped over my easy chair. He pulled the tie off. The fluffy thing flimsily wilted to the floor. He sat across my chest, his very much engorged dick tenting his gray sweatpants and nudging itself between my tits. I had a padded bed frame, so I didn't have the sexy posts to truly make me his prisoner. Nonetheless, he tied my wrists securely with my robe tie.

"I know you can do this. Don't you dare take the easy way out." His usually cheery tenor hit a low rasp. He toyed with the jeweled end of the plug and gave the bulb's end a brief tug. He pushed it back and studied my hips wiggling under his direction. That enticed him to start moving the plug mere centimeters in and out.

Then all the way out.

"What the... Beau?"

He brought the medium-sized plug to my lips. "Warm it up."

I huffed on it, but he gently pushed it past my lips. Once the metal felt warm in my mouth, he coated it in lube and massaged me even more with a few more pumps so I was ridiculously slippery. He gently pushed it against my pleated entrance. Now having been thoroughly worked, it practically sucked the whole thing inside. I didn't wait for him to ask. "You make this feel so good."

He dragged me to the edge of the bed so my butt hovered at the end. He finally ditched his sweatpants and boxer briefs. He ripped open the foil packaging of the condom and put it on. The darkness that had possessed him lifted for a moment. He flickered a boyish grin. "You're my present."

I got it. My wrists were tied in a bow above my head, and I was spread out just for him. It was the sexiest and most powerful I had ever felt, coming off a few weeks of feeling increasingly sexy and powerful.

He entered me only an inch. I felt fuller than when it was just Ole Reliable and the smaller plug. He braced himself with one hand above me, giving me only an inch more. He fucked me in tiny and shallow thrusts. His brows knitted in concentration; his lips held firmly together. He desperately sipped breaths from his nose, the sound of him trying not to lose his mind and use me to the fullest. Yeah, he was being a boss, but this was always about my comfort and fantasy, not his.

"You can go deeper," I said.

His other hand braced against the bed, bracketing my body. He increased the force of his hips. The pressure built in my entire pelvis. I dug my heels into his ass to guide him further. He gripped the comforter on either side of my head. His hips slapped into mine. The sound of skin-to-skin contact heightened everything; I wanted to disappear into it. I squeezed my eyes shut, wanting to memorize the sound of his sighs, the sound of our bodies. The smell of lube, latex, and sex. All of it intoxicating.

"Look at me," he gritted out.

The sudden eye contact pinched his expression into concentration. "You're too good, Sir. Too..." He collapsed into me and stilled, moaning through his climax.

We lay stunned; our hearts drumming back to each other until finally we breathed. All his weight pressing into me felt perfect, comforting.

I looped my arms over his head so I could hold him with every part of me because... because I loved what he did to me... because I loved *him*. Ooh boy, I needed to give myself a serious talk in the mirror because lust and the excitement of being attended to was getting me to feel stupid, foolish, hopeful feelings that should've died when I signed the divorce papers. I had touched the metaphorical stove of catching feels and got burnt. At least my marriage spared my feelings enough by fading into indifference rather than rending me broken-hearted.

"Shit, don't want to leak." Beau sprung off me and removed the condom. As he threw it away in the trash, I removed the plug. Good for us that I had a mountain of toys to run through the dishwasher.

He took his spot on the bed. A warm feeling arrived because at this point, Beau had *his* spot in my bed. Curled against his chest, I got that wistful, teary feeling like I needed to confess something. "Beau, I'm so glad I met you."

He kissed the top of my head. "Same, but you know, me meeting you rather than meeting myself."

"Like our bedroom activities could be easily dismissed as perverted, kinky, depraved, lurid, gross but... it's precious to me." I stopped myself before saying, *You help me realize there's a lot more to life and that I can do anything.*

The beat that passed gave my heart a nervous skip. Had I said something too hokey?

He sighed. "I want to say something profound right now, but I've been fucked stupid."

"Me too," I said. "I cannot be held liable for the cheesiness of the words I said."

But I chided myself in secret because falling for Beau would lead to the violent stumble after. Nope, I was not going to do this again or ever.

But oh shit.

I was completely falling for Beau.

Chapter Twenty-Two

W hen it came to planning a unique yet chal-
lenging cycle class, the trainer became the
trainee. Not gonna lie, I loved having a second set
of one-on-ones in the studio without having to pay
Beau seventy-five bucks a pop. Maybe my sex life
made me more foolish, but I liked entering the gym
after his last class. While others slowly left the
studio to compliment him on a job well done or how
his class changed their whole outlook, I waltzed in,
gloating a bit because I had the real deal: the Beau

who was going to make something of himself and nail this audition.

It wasn't lost on me that one of the familiar members of the cycle divas with the ivory leggings and sports bra with similar ivory-colored hair and ivory shoes scowled as I took a cycle seat while she let the door hit her on the way out. Wasn't she the same woman who scowled at us in the parking lot a while back?

First, Beau showed me the expected playlist. He got to run an entire class for a session as his audition, so he had to run with his best foot forward. Luckily, he had me, a person with taste, for his music consultant. We debated being basic and sunny, settling for top forty standards over the span of the last thirty years. Or going niche—settling on a theme and running with it.

"What do you think of when you think of *me?*" Beau asked as I scanned through an endless list of music.

"You're the dom next door? He tells you what to do, gets you to embrace discomfort, but does it with a mischievous smile on his face?"

"Should that be my class name? The Dom Next Door?"

I was the devil on his shoulder. "Do it."

"Music—Rihanna's 'S & M,' Britney Spears's 'I'm a Slave 4 U.'"

"Or Depeche Mode, Nine Inch Nails, The Stooges, She Wants Revenge, Velvet Underground, Romeo Void."

"I'm nodding because I understand half of what you said."

"Follow my lead, junior."

Once I played him "Never Say Never," he already choreographed a HIIT track to it. It wasn't too hard. He figured out the beats per minute in the music and matched pedaling to it. We got a solid half hour of music that embodied his bossy side and my good taste. Next, we composed a script, optimizing the sexual puns for mass effect.

"Should I use any accessories?"

"What accessories appear in cycling?"

"Water bottle, a towel, sometimes weights."

"Make a pun about needing items from your playroom or something. You could open every class with that."

"This theme is oddly falling into place."

We ran through a speculative script and playlist. I acted the role of a cycling student, and we worked up a sweat. He'd tell me to stand up in a climb; I'd tell him to be bossier.

After working up a sweat in the gym, we rinsed it off at my home. Sometimes we'd work up our own kind of sweat in the sheets, but other times, we just liked eating dessert and watching some Netflix. Really, Netflix and chill.

Bored at work, I drew a sketch of Beau as a cycle instructor combined with a leather daddy. In reality, he probably couldn't lead a class in sunglasses, military boots, and leather shorts. In Beau fashion, the cartoon dom version of him still had his telltale pompadour.

We hit the internet to find the next best thing and make this dom find the right amount of daddy meets suburbia to match his vibe. Imagine our excitement when we discovered cycling boots existed! Actual leather and vinyl would be a bit stifling for sweating and spinning. Together we found some liquid leather–looking Spandex.

"What about the EverGreen & Fit image?" Beau asked me as he assessed whether the slick–looking, black moisture wicking muscle shirt was too dark dom for the fifty shades of green of this gym franchise.

"How about I screen print the logo in a pine green on the black? It will blend in, but it shows that, although you're going for a darker edge, you're not above being corporate. I could use our satin finish to give it a nice sheen, fitting the fake leather and vinyl aesthetic."

My brainchild practically crowning, I finished Beau's shirt first thing at work the next day. I admired the gloss of the dark green against the black.

"I might have some good news for you," Tina sang from the back office.

I carefully folded Beau's shirt so it was a perfect package to give to him.

Tina poked her head out of her office. "Someone expressed interest in bankrolling this place. I'd still have a managerial role, but we wouldn't have to reduce your position or benefits. Maybe even get a better co-pay."

"Cool." As I smoothed one more wrinkle out of Beau's shirt, I realized my exit plan over the last few weeks had been adjusting. If Beau landed the better gig of leading classes on the app, I started devising plans of ditching my condo and following him into the city. Unfortunate flashes of me wearing a wedding ring again and squeezing his hand with a corresponding ring entered my mind as well, but those were girlish wishes. The same ones that said if I lined my locker with my favorite hottie, which happened to be James Iha of the Smashing Pumpkins, that he'd burst through my classroom door and take me on a ride on his flying guitar. Stupid wishes in reality that ended with lawyers and moving boxes. Of course, I convinced myself, I wouldn't be following a man because Beau wasn't my boyfriend.

It was something more than following my heart into San Francisco or living out a song. I'd be pursuing life beyond the dead-end job in Gorda Vista. I had followed my ex-husband across the country. Being conveniently close to Beau was only a forty-five-minute shift in plans. San Francisco offered opportunities I had previously avoided such as using my art to design video games or something for the animation studio nestled in the city.

I had disappeared so far into these visions of the future, I almost missed when Tina said, "Yes, I was at the rotary luncheon and spoke to this guy about investing in a printing business as a way to grow income. He had a name you don't hear often. Perry?"

My stomach flipped at the possibility. The small world of Gorda Vista was shrinking to something even smaller. "Perry Pietraszewski?"

"Yes! Do you know him?"

"All too well," I murmured. There had been conversations where I let Tina know my exaggerated versions of events from the shiny, long tables of law firms. I may have referred to Perry as "The She Demon's Finance Bro with a Respectable Grudge." I wasn't going to deflate her dreams by telling her Finance Bro with a Grudge was Perry.

Chapter Twenty-Three

Another training session hit the books. I schooled my eager student on a crowd-pleasing introduction to some brutal climbs. Beau took notes dutifully, hanging on my every suggestion.

I slung my gym bag over my shoulder. "See you at home?" I bit my tongue and grinned. The unholy things I had planned for Beau and me once we had a shower and a bed.

He quirked his eyebrows. Oh shit. I said *home* as if I implied that my condo was *our* home. With my last relationship being a marriage, I couldn't help but drag him into my old habit.

I murmured, "As in my condo and not Les and Carol's humble abode."

He patted the sweat off his body with the white hand towel, but his gaze lingered on me. "Why can't I see you here?"

The way he said *see*. See meant tearing at my bicycle shorts, driving deep into me. See meant licking along my neck and moaning *good girl* in my ear.

I shifted my focus to my hands—the uneven nails and a splash of ink that couldn't quite wash away. "I thought you said we had to be on our best behavior."

"During open hours." He stepped close while teasing the hem of my T-shirt, the one with the cockatiel. He reached under the hem and grazed his touch along my ribs; his thumb toyed along the sturdy elastic of my sports bra. "I checked the locker room, put the towels in the dryer." He kissed me. The gentle hands under my shirt pulling at the cotton–poly blend became needier and rougher. "I locked the doors."

"Okay, see me then." My voice came out like a croak.

Our kiss deepened. I disappeared in the fierceness of our tongues, the taste of sweat on our lips.

I staggered back. Something poked me! I jumped, clinging to Beau's tank top. "What the—" A bike, he had backed me into a bike.

He slid my shorts down my hips to my ankles and buried his nose in my mons. I whipped my T–shirt off as I watched him sink to his knees and nuzzle my clit that had already been shot to attention from merely kissing him.

And he inhaled. Inhaled all of me. I leaned back on the bicycle seat and moaned. My stance widened to blossom for him. Nuzzle and sniff, that was what he did along my wet folds. Then his lips locked onto me. His tongue and mainly his mouth worked my clit as he tugged my sports bra below my nipples. My boobs were trussed up by the tight elastic support. I closed my eyes to melt into the pleasure and moved my hips toward his mouth the best I could with a stationary bike as my support. *Slap!*

Beau had smacked a boob freed from my sports bra. My entire body curled around him for balance, for relief.

"Whoa, I need a moment." I shook off the bubbles popping in my brain.

He backed away and kneeled on his haunches. "What's up?"

"Maybe we shouldn't do a scene tonight. I can barely drive home if you get me all spacey."

"I'll keep you safe, Sir." He grazed his index finger along the back of my ankle. "Don't you know I will always look out for you?"

The honey usually laced with his commands when we commenced a scene had disappeared. This was *the* Beau offering me not only the rubs, glass of water, and kind words of a dom to a sub in the afterglow. But he himself was giving me safety and kindness beyond the dynamic. The kind of love Chris had revoked.

I peered down at him, his puppy eyes above the tilt of my mons. I nodded. *Bring the heights of this scene. Give more than I can take.*

He slapped my other boob. It prickled alive and turned pink. "Use your words."

"Yes, Daddy?" I looked to him for approval. His nose wrinkled. Beau wasn't a *daddy*. "Yes, sir?" Well, that would get confusing. Finally, the perfect pet name for my young sweet dom popped into my head. "I won't disappoint you, Coach."

He rolled one of my nipples gently between his thumb and index finger. "Good girl."

The sensation beelined from my nipple to my pulsing wet channel. How I needed his fingers, dick, nose, tongue—anything to fuck this ache away. "Give me everything." I tilted my head back, ready to let him feast on me until oblivion.

Another slap across my breast. "No," he rasped, "watch yourself in the mirror."

I set my sights on my reflection, standing yet spread and sloppily naked for him.

"No, you don't see what I need you to see." He kicked a row of bikes down. They toppled like loud dominos. He jerked me to fully standing and moved the bike so it faced parallel to the mirror. The violence of the falling bikes, the fact that he only cared about how much I *needed* to see what he did to me set me in a spin. And spun me higher and higher.

He pushed me back, my ass leaning onto the seat. I braced against the handles and the dainty basket for weights. He spread my folds, pink and glistening. Such details I could not miss even from the distance from the mirror. "Do you see how you get for me?" he asked as he moved his fingers over my labia.

"I only get this way for you," I replied with a sigh.

At those words, he attacked me with his mouth, the bike tipping back with his force. But if I dissolved too much into the pleasure and squeezed my eyes shut? Slap!

He lowered his shorts under the tip of his cock and fisted the dusky shaft as he kneeled before me. "Do you see how much I need you?"

I ran my tongue over my bottom lip, relishing the goddess in the mirror being serviced by her lover. I watched him work the skin up and down over his head, the way his arousal pearled there. "Yes," I said as I smiled wickedly.

"What do you like about yourself, looking in that mirror?"

My gaze moved to him, in a frenzy on the floor. "My eyes."

His hand slapped my inner thigh, a pain stinging evermore because of my sweaty skin. "Look in the mirror," he ordered

"My smile when I'm being a good girl, the bite of my lip when I'm a bad one. How beautiful, raw, and red my nipples get under your touch." From his place on the mat, he met my breasts with kisses and bites. As one nipple pinched between his teeth, my eyes drifted shut. My head tilted back, baring my throat. A twin slap met my other thigh. The pain and pleasure twisted inside me, and I let out a throaty laugh. I stared at myself in the mirror, sweaty and eyes heavy-lidded. "I love these arms that brace me."

"Yes," he hissed before he kissed me on the top of my hand. He resumed stroking himself, his dark eyes watching me in the mirror.

I studied the curve of my belly, the fullness of my hips. Usually, I hated them. They were where life went to die. And they were dimpled, stretch-marked, and sagged. Most days, I wanted to fix them, but as I watched Beau look at them reverently in the mirror, I realized they were gorgeous because this is the part of me that worked him when we fucked. "My belly. My hips. The way I can pulse with you inside. The way I can move my hips to bring you to the brink." He met my words with caresses and kisses. More things I loved about my body tumbled out. "My thighs, my muscular calves because they can hug you close to me." More kisses greeted me in these places. It was as if the more I loved myself, the more love he offered me.

I laughed now, intoxicated by the power I held over him and me. "My feet for balancing me against this damn thing." With one foot at a time, he removed a sneaker and a sweaty sock, kissing the newly exposed, soft, and damp skin.

He slipped his muscle shirt off and tossed it care-
lessly. "Tell me more about your body."

One hand pinched a nipple; the other spread myself out for him, the way he had before as he licked
and lapped at me. "This pussy is going to take
you so good, you'll be coming back for more later
tonight."

He sprang to his feet and moved his way behind
me so our eyes locked as we faced the mirror. We
were separated by the bike's crossbar. "Put your
left foot on the seat," he ordered.

For once, I trusted my muscles and balance, as if
all the work we had done together these last two
months built up my strength to handle now, this
moment. I lifted my leg, propped my foot on the seat,
and hooked my left arm around his neck, becoming
his cycling ballerina.

His eyes didn't move from mine as he presented
the foil of the condom and ripped it open with his
teeth. My gaze latched on the reflection. He had
only inched his shorts below his shaft. I memo-
rized the way his abs twitched as he eased the latex
over him, the way his mouth slacked a bit in what
had to be anticipation.

He smoothed his hand over my extended leg. The
angled crossbar of the bike was not much of a bar-

rier as the head of his cock breached my entrance. "Are you ready?" he asked my reflection.

"Always."

He thrust deeper inside. I fought the need to retreat into myself and breathe, feeling the delightful pinch of him stretching and filling me. I kept my eyes wide open, and I watched. Watched as his thick shaft slipped into me. Watched as his hips met my ass.

"More," I breathed. My grip tightened around the handlebars as he thrust into me. His brows furrowed. His mouth tightened. He muttered curses to himself. "I said more," I purred.

He fisted the hair at the nape of my neck and pulled *hard*. I gasped as I presented my throat to him. To be slayed. To be devoured. However he saw fit. He tugged my hair harder, sending little bursts of joy down my body. The force compounded as he drove into me. Swift. Deep. Devastating. The only way he knew how.

My left leg shook. My gaze moved from the mirror to his. My wide eyes pleaded. I couldn't hold on like this. Thankfully, he let go of my hair. His arm braced me around the waist; the other bolstered my left knee as the force of his thrusts caused the entire bike to teeter. My support leg gave out. But

I didn't fall. He held me in place, driving into me harder. I had become his doll.

Everything around me clouded and vibrated as my eyes rolled to the back of my head. I didn't have it in me to brace my weight any longer. I didn't have it in me to focus on the two of us in the mirror. Any moment now, a slap would surely come to ground me but nothing. He was as lost in the scene as I was.

"Beau, I love—" My entire body tensed and pulsed.

"Yes." He pumped into me grunting.

"I love what you do to me." Everything that had twisted, tensed, and shook finally released. His grip tightened at my hip as he came.

I dropped my leg, and my overworked hamstring throbbed. Heaving inhales and exhales overtook my body. He rested his forehead against my temple. "I've never done anything like that before," he managed to say between panting.

I sank to my hands and knees. He joined me on the ground, kissing my shoulder.

"I guess I bring that out of you." I curled more of my body into him, accepting the whisper of his caresses on my skin.

"You do. Only you do." He enveloped me in his arms.

"But we really should do this with the other leg. Balance and all," I said sleepily. His hug drew me in tighter as he laughed. I begged for my senses not to come to me. I wanted to live in this high forever—to pretend this was love.

We stayed on the mat like that long enough for the auto lights to shut off. In the dark, he crooned, "You're amazing" in my ear. I don't remember when we moved off the floor.

Beau soaked in my bathtub that I loaded with Epsom salt to help ease his muscles. I wiped his eyeliner off using mineral oil, and he finally let out a sigh. "You should join me."

"And get you worked up? You need to relax. I bet you barely have the hip strength right now to thrust."

"I'd lie there and let you do all the work." He looped his wet arm around my legging clad thigh. The water on his hair bled through the fabric on my leg as he nuzzled me. "You've been doing so well with training. I could probably get a second wind if you were up for—" He gave my butt a healthy squeeze.

"Is sex the only thing you have on your mind?"

"It is when I'm around you."

"An answer for everything." I finger combed his coif, his puppy–dog eyes looked up at me. I kissed the top of his head.

"After the audition, we should go somewhere for a weekend. Something along the Pacific Coast Highway or Tahoe."

"That seems…" Fantastic. Great. Perfect. Yes, yes, yes. But feelings and their need to be bubble–wrapped. "Awfully couple–y, isn't it?" I stepped out of his arm loop and patted the wet spot on my leggings with a towel. It was as if his grip had feeling–cooties, and I needed them off me.

"Yeah, but aren't we? The sex, the chores, the helping me with the audition."

"I can care about you without having to make it a whole thing. When you go through a divorce—"

"Sir, you're always thinking five steps ahead. I'm asking for a weekend getaway because we're friends slash lovers and that's what friends–lovers do." He stood up in the bath, the water sluicing over his chiseled body. I made a note of how it flowed out of his belly button to his dick, which was at half–mast. "What I was going to say was you're handling our training so well, I thought you might like to make something special out of—"

"Using my ass?" The way I said it made the act seem crude, the way Chris saw it. As something to be gross and demeaning, not the way things had been when they had been heating up with Beau and not the way he felt so careful and good. The sharp tone of my voice deflated his face and his member.

"I thought you liked it when we—"

"I do. But what happens when the novelty wears off?"

The sexy moments between us were amazing, don't get me wrong, but I longed for those quieter moments of tracing scars on his legs with my fingertips or holding him in my arms after a day of doing chores for his parents. I could be a girlfriend, though the term *girlfriend* belonged to someone younger, bubblier, and armed with a better reproductive system.

"You're more than an amusement to me," he said.

I threw the towel at him. I wanted to tell him that time made us all liars, and I had a proven stanky return on investment in relationships. My ring finger was still pale from years of wearing a wedding ring. I had a past that said feelings got trod upon until I made funny anecdotes about them. I had to be practical about Beau. Beau wasn't going to be a forever person. He was a right-here, right-now one. And as much as he was a fixer, he couldn't fix this one thing about me. "I have to remember why my marriage went to shit."

He stepped out of my tub, laughing and drying himself off. "I'm not your ex."

"I have a bicornuate uterus."

After he wrapped the towel around his waist, he leaned back against my sink and narrowed his eyes, probably trying to figure out what language I spoke.

"I have a heart-shaped uterus. You know, the shape that you dot your *i's* with? It means pregnancies are riskier, and we tried *a lot*. And I went to therapy and learned it wasn't my fault that I was born with something, but when Chris and I went through... one after another..."

He leaped from the counter and held me so close in a ridiculous, damp hug. I could hear his voice through his chest, the comforting low rumble. "I don't dot my *i's* with hearts."

I chuckled.

"I dot them with your uterus. *Saoirse* dotted with your uterus, outlined in your uterus in my notebook."

Only Beau could make something so dark so sweet. It was the type of information that a woman could misinterpret for love. "Making a joke out of my pain, are you?"

His chin rested on the top of my head. "Do you want kids?"

He cut right to it, didn't he? "I think life gave me the answer. There are times I'm grateful I didn't. It made the divorce easier. I look at what Chris's wife had to go through, negotiating custody and what-not... not envious of that. Living alone with my silly job, making my silly doodles, I'm just one big kid. Big kids with my big kid problems don't really have business adding another one to the world."

"Sometimes big kids make the best moms."

I squeezed my mouth shut to hold back from let-ting the pain out—the pain of wanting to be a mom in my other life, a whole other Saoirse ago. Finally, the ache of that came out with a deep breath of the life I had been handed. "What about you?"

He gazed down at me and flickered his adorably crooked smile. "I have a lot of shit to get together before I do any of that. But yes, deep down I'd like to be a dad."

I could already picture it: Him being one of those hot dads at the park who chased his kids, and when he caught them, he zerberted on their tummies as they squealed with laughter. I couldn't take that from him. It didn't matter how many perfect an-swers he had or how good his embrace felt. His answer put an expiration date on whatever we had going on.

I extricated myself from his grip and swallowed back the years of disappointment I had stowed away. "We shouldn't do a weekend getaway. The traffic is atrocious on weekends. And your dad still needs you around as his arm heals."

"Right." His focus went to my ceiling, as if bathroom vents were an actual point of interest. "I should get going. My parents."

He prepared to leave. And as we air kissed each other's cheeks in the threshold of my doorway, I had a feeling that I'd fucked up.

Chapter Twenty-Four

B ack at the shop, paper orders were taking me twice as long to get through since only half of the machine cut like it was supposed to. If I had access to The Mighty Pen bank accounts, I would've scheduled a sharpener yesterday. Tina had stepped off to lunch. And a familiar-looking woman bearing a mountain of card stock flyers came bounding into the store.

"Did *you* do this?" The woman practically threw the pile of flyers at me. They skidded across the counter. Despite having the voice of a witch, she had the best looks money could buy. White-blonde hair with her roots meticulously blended. Skin toned, stretched, Botoxed, and filled to its ideal suppleness. A spray tan that said she loved vacations. And a shape that not only had she bought her ass and hips, but she also had excellent personal training. Too bad the personality didn't match the drapes.

"Hi. What seems to be the problem?" Someone had to be an adult in the room.

"My flyers." She popped a hand on her hip and exasperatedly spread the glossy card stock across the counter with the other. "They're *uneven*."

Tina must've filled this order in a hurry and absent-mindedly let the machine cut with the blunt blades. A keen eye would have caught that the fly-ers sloped. All the more obvious when they were stacked together. They were flyers for an essential oil business, Leanne's. I was assuming this was Leanne.

"I'm really sorry about that. I can reprint the order."

"I had to take time out of my day—"

Just then, *Perry* popped into the store. He had a long, narrow box for a giant stack of business cards under his arm. *Don't tell me those were cut awfully too,* I internally pleaded. He waved sheepishly at me, distracting me from Leanne's tirade.

"I can refund you ten percent on the order." And hurt Tina's bleeding books even more.

"Ten percent? That's what you think my time is worth? Just ten percent?"

"Best I can do is knock off twenty percent." I winced a little, peering into the future where Tina took the hit out of my paycheck. "I'll even have these reprinted and cut in half an hour. You're welcome to wait so you don't have to drive here again."

"Well—" I could tell Leanne wanted to be more pissed. My appeasement immediately disarmed her. The hand on her hip dropped, and she plopped on the seat next to our fake plant, which was added for ambience. "I'll wait."

I held my finger up to Perry to give me a second. I raced to the printer in the back, searched the old order, and clicked *print.* While the order printed, I ran back to the front.

Perry opened the box. Same problem. The cards gradually moved up in height. "I'm really sorry, Sir."

"You didn't print those business cards. We did."

"Tina made this place seem like it ran as smooth as peanut butter."

"It does!" I leaned across the counter, mindful of angry Leanne at the fake plant tapping through her phone. I whispered, "It did. Tina's been cutting corners recently instead of reducing my pay. The paper cutter hasn't been sharpened in a while. Hence, shitty cards and flyers."

"So that's why she's looking for a buyout?"

"Yup."

Perry leaned back and cleared his throat. He said so loudly as if it was an announcement, "Mistakes happen. You don't have to refund anything. Oh hi, Leanne. Nice seeing you." They were on a first name basis because of course, we lived in the smallest suburban enclave in the East Bay.

"Perry, nice to see you." Leanne forced a smile for enough microseconds until Perry looked away. She rolled her eyes and returned to the far more interesting task on her phone. It was lovely what one can see from the perspective of the work counter.

"I thought we'd see each other more after that wild cycle ride."

Right, I had been busy getting the Beau Bishop special seven days a week. "I've been trying to keep this place afloat," I said quietly, not to give Leanne any ideas. But I'd been busy with double duties: setting an order on print and fucking my personal trainer in the alley on a stack of boxes.

"If I buy this place, are you part of the deal?" Perry asked. There was a shimmer to his gaze that was far more flirtatious than I had ever remembered in our encounters. From the mansplaining in the gym, the giddiness after the cycle session, and now—if I didn't know any better—Perry Pietraszewski was trying to date me.

I deflected in my charming Midwest way. Playing gullible and stupid so not to sour a relationship with a would-be check signer. "Oh, Tina's mentioned some changes. I don't know. Maybe it's time I pack up and head to the city." *Maybe even try to be a real artist again.* "I've had more Chris and Claire sightings in the last couple of months than I had in almost eighteen. I think Gorda Vista is getting a little small."

"You wouldn't pack up and go into the city, Sir. At our age?"

Shit, Perry, I wanted to say. Given the average lifespan of privileged Americans such as ourselves, I'm not even at a halfway point when it comes to life. I'm supposed to stay in one place? "You know what they say, Per, age is just a number."

"You're hilarious, Sir. That's what I like about you. Do you want to discuss business over some drinks tomorrow?"

Tomorrow Beau had his audition. After he'd re-turn on the train at the tail-end of rush hour, we planned on debriefing the nightmare and read-ing smut to each other out loud. "Thanks, really. I just made plans with a friend is all." The word *friend* caught in my throat. I wished in that mo-ment I could say "boyfriend, my S.O., partner." Due to dumbassery in the name of self-protection, I couldn't.

"A later date then. My number is on those mis-shapen business cards. Call me when you're free."

"I'll have these reprinted by this evening. I promise."

"I'm not worried about those, Sir."

Perry left.

Leanne rested her phone in her lap. "I recognize you from somewhere."

"Probably here. Gorda Vista is small." And seeming to get smaller by the minute.

"No, do you work out at that obnoxiously green gym?"

"EverGreen & Fit Studios?" I asked.

"That's where I know you from!"

Shit, shitting, shit. Leanne was one of the front row cycle divas. The scowler who had it out for me ever since I fell out of my car and Beau slapped my ass. "Oh right."

She stood up and sauntered back to the counter. "I know this might not be any of my business, but are you Beau Bishop's new *friend?*"

The way she said *new friend* gave me a sick feeling—like being labeled side piece, concubine, the other woman. "Yes. We're friends."

"Let me guess. He charmed you into hiring him for personal training, and the session got a little more *personal* than *training?*"

My hands grew clammy. "I don't feel comfort-able—"

"Girl to girl? He goes after women like us as if we're wounded deer. I was in a separation when I started training sessions. Things took a sexy turn, but when he found out I wasn't getting anything in my divorce, he chilled considerably. You know he lives with his parents, right?"

If I moved, I'd puke. Shock wasn't the right word for the feeling. I knew the truth. I knew it from the very beginning. The strange personal invest-ment he had in me when we met; the way he asked about my divorce and wedged himself inside all my personal details. He never stopped taking my money, even when things became a bit dubious on the training front. He didn't want me. He wanted my alimony. And where was he going to be in three years when that eventually dried up? I blinked. Blinked to acknowledge I heard Leanne.

"Are you separated? Divorced?"

"D–d–divorced," I murmured.

"Well–off ex? Getting alimony?"

I nodded. "For a few more years, at least." Quiet enveloped the shop. I lost myself in the repetitive whir of the printer in back. It suddenly stopped. "I need to go cut your flyers."

"That can wait, honey. I think the fumes in here are getting to me. Would you like to join me for a coffee or something?"

"I can't leave the shop while the manager is out."

"Too bad. I could bring something back for you." She must've seen me grab at my stomach. "Something herbal?"

"A mint tea would be nice."

"I'll be back in half an hour." She paused in the doorway. "Even when things didn't work out, he still was a blast in class. He's one of the best trainers around here. It's why I couldn't leave the gym."

Once she left, I cut her flyers, anger slicing and stacking. I boxed and taped them, added The Mighty Pen logo sticker, and gave the package one last spin on the counter before the new order was ready to go. I clicked the next order for printing. The murmur of the printer kicked in. I bent over the counter, propping myself up on my elbows.

I had made it my goal to wrap my heart in bubble wrap, to make sure my feelings were safe and protected like the order of "The Birthday Bitch" wine glasses I had next on the order queue. I blamed our physical intimacy for chipping away at my guard. Devastating orgasms pierced through any armor of common sense. Beyond that, other things played out in my brain. The sweet things he said. The way he tilted his head all the way back when he ate noodles. The way he danced and flipped pancakes to Carly Rae Jepsen songs. The way I laughed with him. All lies, a performance to suck me in.

When Chris had asked for a divorce, the first words out my mouth was, "That tracks." When he and Claire premiered as a couple, I said, "Of course." After the third miscarriage, Chris had to go for a long walk. I flatly asked, "What else did you expect?" I hadn't cried. I had no tears left.

But today, I went for it. Snotty, messy tears that bled into my shirt sleeve. Sobs that echoed off the printing room walls and bounced off the machines. My therapist had said my under reactions were a sign I wasn't giving my emotions any room. If I wasn't going to make time for them in the present, they were going to come up later in something else. "Like divorce?" I had asked. Never got a response.

That evening, Beau was going to try his entire Dom Next Door program officially in a cycle class at the studio as a practice run for his audition. I had planned to be front and center, to *woo* my heart out for him. Instead, I texted.

> Hey, big order came up at work :(Can't come tonight

> I'll come over after class and tell you all about it :D

He arrived at my apartment, adorably still dressed in his audition outfit and eyes outlined in black. The zip-up hoodie he wore for warmth was draped open. His horn-rimmed glasses perched on his nose.

I let him in. I had spent the evening finishing what I had left of some amaretto and sobbing into my sleeve. Not exactly handling last-minute orders as I had led him to believe.

"The class was an absolute hit. I wish you'd been there. I think I need to work on my timing with this one pun, but I'll smooth it out before the audition."

I let him drone on as I filled my plastic juice cup with more amaretto.

"This might seem a little gross, but you have got to check out what I found on my mom's bookshelf." He fished a beat-up paperback from his hoodie pocket. *Delightfully Pursued by the Duke and Prince.* "I saw the passages the cracks in the binding automatically opened to. We're in for an exciting night." I squirmed out of his arms, which reached for my waist. "You smell like you've been through half a liquor cabinet. Work going that badly?"

The alcohol in my system flicked off my doubts, telling me to back down. "So many times I've asked 'Why me? Why did he pick me?' This town is practically teeming with divorced first wives, and I've seen them. They can do that leg thing over their head and have weaves of lush hair to their asses. Divorces and young personal trainers look good on them."

He squinted in confusion.

"I talked to Leanne." I gestured with the cup, sloshing sweet liquor onto the floor. "Blonde gym-goer with the hottest ass money could buy?"

"I know Leanne." He clenched his jaw and stood with his hands in his hoodie pocket, waiting for the other shoe I was going to drop.

"The pattern she described to me was so fucking familiar. Hot trainer with a disarming personality cheers up an older divorced woman who buys lots of one-on-one sessions. They turn sexual. Over a cup of tea, she showed me the social media profiles of Beth and Liz. A familiar face popped up in all of them." The mint tea and air-dirty-laundry session with Leanne had unearthed a sickening number of social media photos. It was just as infuriating realizing none of his exes hated him enough to delete or untag a photo. They were proud he was a notch on their post.

His normal sunny expression burnt out into a blank. "We're grown-ups, Sir. I have a past."

"Not just any past. You're a fucking shark. A shark that bails when the money source dries up!"

"Interesting take. Did Leanne tell you that she dumped me when she found out I lived with my parents? Or that Beth went back to her marriage? And Liz is on her second marriage to a retired periodontist!"

"And those are the ones still going to the gym! Leanne said there was a huge turnover in cycle class not too long ago. No wonder they advertise

21

free first classes. Their star instructor keeps shitting where he eats." It was like the fake drawing all
over again. I had a winner, but it turned out Beau
was the human equivalent of the free coupon given
to every new customer. Why didn't I just take a free
koozie?

"I've made mistakes, but I swear, Sir, with you—"

"With me it's different, huh? Because I'm a lonely
ol' loser who doesn't care you didn't go to college or
you live with your parents. Ply me with enough sex
and conversation, and I'll tolerate anything, right?"

His chin trembled, the unflappable finally flap-
ping. "I'm in love with you, Sir. I wanted to make
the moment I said it special this weekend. But you
need to know it now. I love you."

I had heard this before. Along with words like *I
do* and *for better or worse.* I had enough lawyer-led
meetings and signed documents to know that
words themselves meant nothing. "Bullshit."

"It's not bullshit. I love you."

My right knee buckled. The way he said it was
what any woman wished to hear, a master class
delivery. It's almost like he had majored in acting
in college. "You'll say anything for the money."

"It's not like that."

"Then why am I still paying you? Seventy-five buckaroos, five times a week." Admitted sex workers were cheaper and probably had better ethics.

His gaze drifted to the floor. "The optics are not ideal."

"Yeah, no shit."

"I should've stopped taking your money. I know. But the increase in training sessions and class attendance caught corporate's attention. I couldn't have this audition without you, Sir, in more ways than one."

"So, you used me."

"I didn't mean—I love you."

"You convinced me you weren't a dumb jock, Beau, but all this time you've been worried about auditioning for the app, you could've used your actual talent and just jerked it on the FanTasy app for five times that amount."

His face turned to stone. "I'm not a prostitute."

"Then why do I feel like a john?" My bottom of the liquor cabinet amaretto was finished. That left an embarrassingly old bottle of Baileys for the next drink of choice to drown my sorrows in. "I called Margie at the front desk to cancel my membership. She directed me to a stupid 1–800 number. I was on hold for over an hour, so I just called my bank and canceled my card. Your gym really is a piece of shit." I poured myself the Baileys and shambled to the front door, opening it.

"So this is over." He began his exit but paused in the doorway. "You're a quitter, Sir. It's true when you work out, and it's true with us. You wanted to go with the flow and not label this?" He gestured a two-way street between us. "Because you'll do anything to make quitting easier."

"Another *boy* with another shitty opinion. I'd suggest you stop fucking divorced women, Beau. We're like the Olympians of quitting because we know a rigged game isn't worth playing."

He nodded and closed the door behind him.

At first, the crying came out like a cough, a little something stuck in my throat. I stopped my mouth with the back of my hand. Waterworks poured from my eyes. Another held back cry and snot shot out of my nose. I ran to my bed and collapsed into it. All this time, I thought I had put my feelings in the equivalent of a black box on an airplane. These things were supposed to survive the inevitable crash. But no. My stupid feelings caused the crash, as if they were a taunting gremlin perched on the wing.

Chapter Twenty-Five

I woke up the next morning with an actual hangover and a crying hangover. My eyes could barely open. Cucumber-infused eye patches were not enough to brighten them up. I floated into work in a daze, surviving on coffee and ibuprofen.

If Beau was a lie, then this funk could be a lie too. I selected *Perry* on my phone and sent him a text.

> Actually my plans fell through :) Want to talk business over drinks tonight?

The three dots pulsed immediately. He read it and was considering an answer. Then nothing. Shit, shitting, shit. I guess I was only alluring to Perry when I had been Beau's fuckee. The universe sent the message out. *Saoirse Hooper is a Bag of Shit!*

Ten minutes later, *ding!* I got a text message.

See you at Vine and Spirits at 7

That's where Beau and I went after the book signing. And he had the audition today. A part of me worried I'd sent him off his game with an ill-timed breakup, but we weren't exactly together. The other part wondered if frauds even had feelings. He did look sad when he left, but that was acting.

How does one get ready for cocktails when they feel like shit? They choose materials that feel like pajamas but look high-end. That's how I ended up in a jersey knit fit and flare dress and a cardigan with squirrels stitched all over it. Again, not one of my designs. No amount of eye makeup gave my cried-out, prune-feeling eyes a rested and happy appearance.

Perry, like Chris, showed up looking like he was about ready to captain a ship. Claire had a type.

He pulled out my bar stool for me. "I've seen you around the gym. You're always with that personal trainer. It looks like the sessions are really paying off."

I forced a smile and took off my squirrel cardigan, fishing for more compliments. "I'd recommend him but there's a chance he'll be moving to a different gym."

"Maybe *we* can work out together."

"Yeah. Maybe." I wished I could bring out a slideshow presentation to show Perry how he had the best way of causing my wounds to fester. Luckily, the bartender came to take our drink orders before I screamed. Exhausted, I ordered the espresso martini as a pick me up.

Perry chuckled, sounding nervous. "That caffeine would keep me up at night."

I needed the caffeine to feel alive. "C'mon, don't you want to stay up all night?" I schmoozed using one of Beau's lines.

"I'm coaching kid's soccer tomorrow, and I'd hate to do that groggy. I'll keep things simple with a pilsner. Have you been to the Hopsy and Flopsy Brewery?"

I helped that brewery print a whole bunch of items for a promotional booth during Oktoberfest. None of the free samples they offered me registered as remarkable, just fizzy, foamy, beer-tasting beer. "I printed banners for them." I hoped to turn the conversation to business after my bad flirtation fell flat. I sipped my martini and rubbed my knee, longing for the playful nudge I'd get from Beau at this point.

"Ah yes, The Mighty Pen. I looked at the books. It's not really the finances that are Tina's issue. She wants out of the business. If I keep you and hire a few part-timers, I'd recoup the amount of debt I'd get into in no time." He took a long series of chugs from his beer and sighed. "But I lied. I said I wanted to talk about business, but that isn't true."

I tucked my hair behind my ear and forced a smile. Maybe I'd finally get the ego boost I was seeking.

Perry reached inside his blazer and brought out a yellow envelope folded in half. "The law firm that settled the divorce didn't do all the research I demanded. I hired a private eye."

The blood in my face dropped to my toes. "Why would you do something like that?"

"Because they denied it, and they made out of the whole thing unscathed, waltzing around town as if they're frickin' Ryan Reynolds and Blake Lively. *They* get to be *happy?* Shouldn't they have to feel an iota of the misery they put us through?" Perry practically shook as he fidgeted with the seal of the envelope. He had printed a stack of screenshots.

The sip on my martini turned into a full-blown gulp. The bartender took that as a cue to offer another one. *Please.*

"They said they never cheated. That the high school reunion took them by surprise." He pounded his finger in the middle of the screenshots. "My private eye was able to find direct messages off social media."

My stomach churned. Not because this completely reshaped how I viewed Chris and Claire, but because the screenshots invaded their privacy, regardless of how someone claimed we gave up privacy using social media. Perry could pile thousands of DMs that documented the start of their nefarious affair, but would it change where I was at this point? Did it change the roommate situation our love had faded into? My indifference shriveled me on the inside, taking someone with the strength of Beau to get me to open up and feel. Maybe I could finagle a discount on rent from my landlord/ex with some salacious info, but I didn't want to relive the inside of law firms and the paperwork. Then the real victim of this rehashing flashed into my mind, Claire and Perry's kid.

"Does Maverick know?" I asked.

"That his mother chose your husband over our family? Not yet."

I wanted to wring Perry's neck. *Don't say that to your kid. Don't vilify his mom like that.* I might not like how Claire and Chris began, if I was going to give scanning those printed screen shots an ounce of room in my life, but Maverick deserved to be free of the bullshit.

"Actually, I cheated first."

Beer foam flew from Perry's lips. He continued to sputter.

"Yup, with the personal trainer you saw me with. I joined that gym and couldn't keep my hands off his young, muscular body. Chris tried to work it out after I confessed the affair. But, no, I could not stop. Chris didn't bring it up in the divorce proceedings because he's a good one. Those DMs, which I've seen, would be a guy just trying to break through his loneliness with an old friend."

Perry sighed and stared at the streaks of beer at the bottom of his glass. "You started it."

"Shamelessly. And if we go through more hoopla with my spanky, choke-happy laundry airing, I might lose a housing situation."

"I wouldn't want to put you through that. But an affair? Really, Sir?"

"Have you seen Beau Bishop?" Images of sexy Beau appeared in my memory, the muscles, the fit of his bike shorts, his warmth underneath me. The sexy images bled into the quiet moments, the way he kissed the top of my head when he told me I could be a good mom. The way he helped me break through my fear and get a signed copy from Preeti. The way he joined me on my smut and face mask nights. Sure, it was a lie; a lie that lifted me, so I wasn't some bitter crone trying to focus on how I was victimized by the past. I finished my espresso martini and paid for the drinks. "The best revenge, Perry, is being happy."

And I left the bar for home. In the comfort of my pajamas, in layers of moisturizer, I opened a fresh new book of smut, living my best life. I made it past one description of the book's love interest—flat, plane of a stomach—and I threw it across my bed.

I missed Beau already.

Chapter Twenty-Six

My meeting with Perry had disastrous con-
sequences. I showed up to work after the
weekend with Tina in full panic mode. Her wonder
investor from the Rotary lunch backed out. It made
me wonder if Perry was going to buy an entire
printing business to purchase my loyalty to his
side. When I wasn't going to easily stab Chris and
Claire in the front, I was no longer an ally. In fact,
my fictional slutty ways may have usurped Chris
from the antagonist role.

When Tina reported that starting the next pay cycle, I'd definitely have reduced hours and needed to be mindful of the next open enrollment period with health insurance, I blocked the gibberish out. It would be foolish to head toward the city.

To Beau.

Beau had his audition before the weekend, and I had no idea how it worked out. I was tempted to send him a text, but with the way I ended things, I'm sure his response would be *Leave me alone.*

Maybe I should do what I should've done in the first place after the divorce, head back to the Midwest with my tail between my legs. Fiona would enjoy it. She could pawn Mom and her problems off on me. I could even save a hefty sum living with Mom for a while. It was even possible in the Midwest that a loser like me could actually own a home and didn't have to once be in a sexual relationship with her landlord for some rent control.

Tina hugged me and cried, whimpering about how she ruined my life.

Her tears stained my dead possum apron. "You're handling this so well."

"I..."

She buried her face in my canvas adorned bosom, ugly crying. I hugged her back, as tight as a hug from Beau. Those close hugs in which you're not sure whose heartbeat was whose.

Everyone thought I took everything so well: the loneliness I found in my marriage that drawing my existential crisis critters chased away and the pain of losing one pregnancy after another and another. I handled it with a shrug and a joke. Maybe if I was supposed to have a kid, I wasn't supposed to have a fucked-up uterus.

I breathed in Tina's scent, a powdery floral perfume mixed with the ever-present smell of ink. I didn't fight the divorce. Because I assumed I had a healthier viewpoint than Perry, I wasn't going to hold a grudge and be out for revenge.

But my lack of fighting was something else. I didn't think the love I offered was worth fighting for or worth feeling the disappointment of rejection. I had stopped creating cartoons because I was making a cartoon of myself—one foot in the door, the other turned to make an exit. I ran away from the Midwest, but I also ran away from my feelings.

I didn't like how Beau called me out like that. On the next exhale, I joined Tina sobbing. By the time we finished, I'm sure I had made my past therapist proud. I made room for my feelings. It even cleared my head a bit.

I was going to be okay with reduced hours. I wasn't going to be cut off yet from the alimony, which gave me time to consider my second act. I went home that evening, ate a few crackers with peanut butter, sat at my easel, and drew. I warmed up with a *Dead on the Inside and the Outside* dead possum. I redrew the drawing of Beau as a physical therapist except I drew the spine model he held up like it had been freshly ripped from a human body, ink blots of blood everywhere. Juvenile but I was getting warmer.

From the comedic blood, I thought of the blood from my miscarriages. I drew a cartoon version of myself, curled on the floor of the bathroom, head resting on my knees. I added a thought bubble, *Don't look in the toilet.* The next image, Beau holding me in the bathroom. The cartoon says, *Sometimes big kids make the best moms.* The next drawing got meta. A drawing of me drawing.

The next frame, a baby popped off the page. It walked, stood fully upright, and talked. "You stole this idea from *Ally McBeal,*" the baby announced.

"Alright, kid," cartoon me said, "*let's fuck shit up.*" My final drawing of the night was me and the baby dancing in my kitchen, flipping pancakes in the air and on all the surfaces.

I woke up in the middle of the night, my condo so quiet I could hear the gurgle of the hot tub outside. Ink stained my cheek, but from looking at the scattered images, I knew what to build out of my empire of mediocrity.

Already the winds were changing. I had to double dose my allergy medicine to make it through the bursts of pollen in the air. Apart from the romantic wound I had been nursing, I missed cycling, the music, the high fives from the *woo* ladies. I made up for it with brisk walks, walks I soundtracked to my elder millennial angst of alternative rock and even that pop punk drivel I was too cool for. I still was a contrarian shit.

The stretches and core workouts I stopped getting under the guidance of the EverGreen & Fit Studios, I performed in the comfort of my living room right before I sat down and drew my stories. Instead of ink, I returned to drawing on my digital pad. I drew vignettes from my life such as the one about sleeping with my decade-younger personal trainer, dealing with run-ins of Chris and Claire, the jellyfish sting of every conversation with Perry bringing up any painful memory. With enough accumulated in my collection, I dusted off my old social media account and uploaded the tale of winning a drawing, which led to the shittiest initial experience at the gym. The last image was a shining, perfect drawing of Beau, savior of souls.

I marked it with a handful of hashtags to make it findable. I'm sure Perry had some kind of search engine optimization he'd recommend. But I needed to do this for myself. Maybe the only people who'd see it were Fiona and me. But maybe someone out there wanted to find solace in my silly, little drawings.

Chapter Twenty-Seven

I was in the midst of finishing my mission of delivering a screen-printed table skirt to a realtor in an enclave of small businesses and office suites. On the sidewalk, I noticed a bunch of garish yellow balloons under a similarly jaundiced awning. "Do you like your current gym?" a baby-faced woman holding a clipboard called after me as I walked by.

I stopped mid stride. "What?"

"Do you like your current gym? I can tell by the way you move that you work out."

"Are you hitting on me?"

"No, um, I work for Goin' Bananas Gym." She sliced her hand through the air to indicate the nonstop yellow. Get it? The obnoxious branding? "What does your current gym offer?"

"I don't have a current gym."

"Would you like to try our special introductory offer for new clients?"

Oh, a bullshit promotion to get me to believe I was special. "What's the offer?"

"A free *week*. You can attend one class a day and have unlimited access to the weight and cardio room for a week."

"Neato."

"You need to fill out this form."

Of course. The form asked for name, address, and a credit card. I gave the number of the one I recently canceled.

"You can sign up for the classes you want to go to online. That way, you're always guaranteed a spot."

And before I knew it, I was signed for a week of free classes at the Goin' Bananas Gym.

The next day, I arrived at the gym wearing my good luck lavender bike short set with the matching sports bra. I wore the chemical-burn, accidental crop top with the cat and toys—the *pussy* one. I signed in at the desk. "I'm here to take Balletch with

Jackie." Balletch being the lovely portmanteau of ballet and stretch, a Goin' Bananas exclusive exercise class.

"You can't wear that shirt here," the teen at the front desk said. I'd call him Killjoy Kyle.

I gave the cartoon on my boobs a look over. "Really?"

"We want to keep the place family friendly."

"I can turn it inside out?"

"You're welcome to purchase one of our shirts."

That's how I found myself in a Balletch class in a yellow shirt with a giant peeled banana on it. Having to deal with an unexpected shirt problem, I was one of the last to arrive in class. Front and center.

The rest of the Balletch classmates wore black unitards and easily had a lot more height than me. Did I just walk in on a ballet class for adults?

"This is Jackie's class, right?" I asked.

"Yes, she's fantastic," the retired ballerina to my right said. She even had the bun and the wrap sweater that screamed she'd burnt a hole through her disc copy of *Center Stage*.

Jackie padded in. She wore shiny, black leggings with a yellow sports bra, and a matching yellow scrunchie held her ponytail back. Her stance was in perpetual turn out. In a soothing voice, she greeted, "Hi, ladies. Welcome to intermediate Balletch. We have something for everyone. To the beginners who are trying us out for the first time—hi, Sah-oy-ers. Cute shirt."

I murmured that my name was pronounced *Sir-sha*. And didn't she realize the yellow monstrosity was the gym's own creation? I wouldn't wear a half-peeled banana without some kind of dick joke scrawled underneath. Maybe some anti-circumcision rallying cry—*Don't snip the tip*.

"Let's warm up." Jackie lay down on the mat. I followed suit. She held her legs up at a forty-five-degree angle, tipped her chin to her chest, and flapped her arms while she breathed something out of a birthing class.

I did my best to copy Jackie.

"Relax your shoulders, Sah-oy-ers. Keep the movement of your arms between the floor and your shoulders. Feel that pulse, Sah-oy-ers?"

"Just call me Sir," I grunted, sounding more like a toad.

We completed a few more exercises in which I appeared to be backstroking through the air confused. My face contorted into distressed expressions in the mirror. My muscles didn't feel jack or shit, but apparently if I kept my movement within my hip socket—whatever the fuck that meant—I'd feel the burn in my glute.

On top of confusion came lies. "Let's work for those long, lean arms we all love about Balletch."

Muscles didn't lengthen. A long and lean look was achieved in the kitchen, not the gym. If Jackie had a personal trainer like Beau, she'd know that.

Then came the pièce de résistance, shoulder stands. My core strength had improved since my first foray into lifting my ass above my head. It also helped to have an extrinsic motivation—how easily Beau could pile drive me with his cock in bed was a perfect motivator. I sat up, watching all the ballerinas effortlessly whoosh their legs above their heads, toes hitting the floor above their head.

"Go for it, Sah-oy-ers!" Thighs crushing her diaphragm deflated Jackie's enthusiasm from her voice.

I looked around the room to find a supply closet or a cart of accessories. "Call me Sir. Do you have any bolsters or anything?"

"Reliance on accessories can weaken your practice."

What a giant load of horse shit. "Cool, so do you?"

"Just go for it!"

I swung my legs over my head; my boobs crushed my throat. In a room full of elegant swans, I was a waddling duck kicking the air for dear life. And like some kind of cartoon duck, I grunted out a request. "How... can... I... breathe?"

"Normally, you don't want that much swing. It becomes less of a core strengthener then. Straighten your legs." Annoyance threaded Jackie's tone. I was a less-than-ideal student, and she was the teacher who possessed a withering iota of patience for me.

"Boobs... crushing... me." My tits pressed into my voice box.

Jackie returned with a singsong, "You got this, Sah-oy-ers."

I rolled out of the mess. I had a middle finger and two legs. And I walked out.

I was hoofing it on my way home, loving the post-workout injustice huff I had driven myself into. A tan sedan slowed down next to me as I walked along the sidewalk. Was I going to get kidnapped?

"Sir!" a woman's voice called out.

I turned to see Beau's mom, driving her car at a crawl. "Good, I recognized you from the wild shirt."

Didn't want to break it to her that this one wasn't *mine*.

"Hi, um, Mrs. Bishop."

"Oh for fuck's sake, call me Carol." Who would've thought Beau's progenitor could be so lovingly exasperated? She continued, "We inferred something happened between you and Beau when you stopped coming around."

I might have played the part of a girlfriend, showing up randomly at their house. I didn't have the heart to tell her our relationship was transactional. Cash for ass. "Beau and I weren't really—"

"He nailed the audition and accepted a job offer in San Francisco. I barely see him now. He leaves in the morning, returns later at night."

He did it. In the way that I knew he would. I held the corners of my mouth together to keep my smile from beaming.

"Have you had lunch yet?"

I hadn't. But me, rounding forty, wasn't going to rely on my ex-lover's mother's kitchen. "Um..." *Must think of an excuse faster.*

"Get in the car."

Did Beau get his dom side from his mom? Jesus! Of course I slid into the passenger seat.

She fixed me the same lunch my mom packed me when I was twelve. A turkey sandwich, baby carrots, apple slices, a chocolate chip cookie, and a tall glass of skim milk. She asked me how long I had lived in the area—eight years; what brought me here from the Midwest—my then-husband's job, now ex-husband.

I ate the last crumb of the cookie. Honestly, with how good it tasted, I was surprised Beau had the body fat levels he did.

"Can I show you something?" Carol asked.

"Um..." This woman left me as speechless as her son.

"Beau won't be here for a few more hours in case you're worried you'll have an awkward run-in." She waved her hand for me to follow her.

We entered his bedroom. It was clean with blue-gray carpet and matching plaid comforter tucked impeccably over a single bed. He had a Foster the People poster on his wall. My presence invaded this museum of adolescence. I was seeing a side of Beau that I had no right to see. Carol gestured to a picture frame on his cherry wood dresser drawers.

I bent to take a look. It was the cocktail napkin from the night I got Preeti's autograph. He had framed it. I had drawn on the napkin to be silly and disposable like most of my ideas. That my silliness turned him sentimental lit internal fireworks. "I'll be damned."

His sentiment hit me harder than a cartoon piano. This meant… Beau loved me. Maybe not now, but he did once, and I ran his feelings through a paper shredder.

"Thank you for showing me this," I said.

She shrugged. What had he told her about us?

"He said he loved me. I didn't believe him," I confessed.

Carol crossed her arms over her chest. "He majored in acting because someone thought he was cute. He wasn't *that* good at it."

I gaped at her, not sure if her brutal honesty made her the world's worst or best mom.

"He hasn't started filming for the app yet. He's spending the first month teaching classes at the San Francisco gym. That is if you want to know where to find him." A knowing smirk emerged from her lips. I'd seen a similar quirk of the mouth from Beau, usually when he was being smart and cute at the same time. Carol was meddling alright.

That night, I drew a picture of me and the cartoon baby swinging on some swings in Sequoia Station Park. We faced the sun set, our backs to the viewer. My speech bubble said, *I think I fucked up my second chance at love.*

A situation like this needs a grand gesture, the baby answered. The next frame, the baby spread its arms and smiled, facing the viewer. *How about changing your own diapers!*

After I uploaded that cartoon to my social media account, I had a notification, which told me more traffic than usual came to my page. Apparently, the cartoon where I embarrassed myself in front of a professional illustrator took off. It latched on to a few millennials in arrested development meme compilations, and I was finally getting my art viewed. One comment read, *I need this on a T-shirt.*

But my favorite hearts of them all came from a username *littlebeaublue.* He liked the one where I made a personal trainer look like a shining superhero saving me from the doldrums of a corporate gym.

I continued to draw until my eyelids drooped. The last drawing was me and the baby under the shade of a sycamore tree. *I think I love him too.*

When I love something, I never let it go, the baby said. The next frame, it was back in the grass, baby feet displayed for the reader to see. *Either that or I puke on them.*

It took the cartoon manifestation of my baby, but I realized I loved Beau too. Did he still love me?

It would take a grand gesture.

Chapter Twenty-Eight

I trained for this moment like I was fucking Rocky. I jogged on trails. Or jogged, then briskly walked. Or briskly walked, then sauntered. I attempted unmodified push-ups until I had to accept I needed to do the modified push-up. I performed full sit-ups until I gave up and settled on crunches. I was going to attend one of Beau's classes and make it my bitch.

I rode the rapid transit all the way into San Francisco. The most difficult leg of my journey was dealing with the front desk person again. Who knew I'd have to go through the whole rigamarole just because I canceled my membership? I forked over my credit card. *Dammit, take my money Ever-Green & Fit Studios.*

"It looks like you're signed up for our Advanced Cycle Boot Camp class. We want to make sure our clients are prepared for the level of difficulty this class provides."

"Does Beau Bishop teach this class?"

"Yes."

"Then it will be right up my alley."

I showed up fifteen minutes early inside the studio, a room so oppressively dark green from floor to ceiling, I thought I had stepped inside a photo development lab. Bikes and mats had been positioned on three sides of a slightly raised platform in front of a wall-sized mirror. On top of the platform was a lone bike and mat. That was the instructor's area, where Beau would be. I selected my bike, front and center, and double-checked I had all my equipment: kettlebell, full water bottle, hand towel. I adjusted my bike the way Beau had taught me. I clipped in and did a few jogs and climbs on the bike. Whatever Beau Bishop threw at me, I was going to throw right back.

More people arrived in the gym, laying out their workout area next to the bike. They looked like triathletes, tall, sinewy people who did outrageous things like swim across bodies of water or hike multiple days in the mountains.

Maybe I could wait for Beau outside of class. I started to unclip from the bike.

The lights dimmed. I was in the dark. A spotlight beamed toward the stage. Beau emerged from the depths of the darkened room. He wasn't the cycle daddy character we came up with. He was just normal ole Beau.

"Hello, my current Evergreen family and those new to my cycle crew. Welcome to advanced boot camp. If you're new, bootcamp will baptize you by fire, but don't you worry, I have an amazing plan for you. We'll combine some tough climbs and intervals on the bike with some fast-paced strength training to raise your heart rate and spirits and push you to your physical limits. If you're ready to become a Beau Bishop Baddie, can you make some noise?"

I wooed as loudly as a woman who was about three goblets into a bottle of rosé. Beau squinted. One part near sightedness, the other part staring directly at a spotlight. Did he recognize me by a *woo?*

The warm-up, jog, and climb were painless and set to some forgettable, radio-friendly electronic dance music. Those intervals were my bitch. We unclipped from our bikes and changed shoes for strength training. The lights came up as we switched shoes. I was tying my red skater shoes on my foot when Beau made eye contact with me. At first, he looked like he had just smelled shit, a valid reaction to me. Then his expression melted into a tiny smile. I returned the expression.

The full body workouts were going fine. Nothing but squats into overhead pulls and deadlifts into rows. I had a healthy sweat going on. Maybe all the hard work I completed over the last few months made me the equivalent of these triathletes.

Beau signaled for us to switch our shoes back. Once we did, we clipped back into the bikes, and Beau said the evilest thing I had ever heard. "Resistance at fifty with an RPM of ninety." Not impossible but the feeling of marching in taffy. Surely those numbers were a mistake. Then he announced it again, as if he knew I was on the verge of asking. Yes. Evil. At least he set it to some good, late-period Weezer.

I focused on my breath, trying to keep myself from panting like a tired dog already. Through the nose, I reminded myself. Beau riffed about the song's "memorable music video," which consisted of icons "from the old internet days like Cara Cunningham, Kelly, and the Numa Numa guy."

"Some of you folks out there know what I'm talking about."

"You bet," a proud elder millennial shouted across the room.

I'd join him in enthusiasm if I wasn't trying to figure out how to breathe and move my legs at such a wicked level of resistance. Beau finally announced a flat road to the song "Steal my Sunshine." Easy. Then a minor key electronic song by the Prodigy kicked in. We were doing cycle sprints of 120 RPM with a resistance of forty. My heart was going to puke itself out of my chest.

Finally, we were back on the mat, changing into our normal shoes again. But the evil kept evilling. Front lunge, back lunge, right side lunge, left side lunge, repeat. By the time I was finished with one round, Beau and the triathletes had lapped me by four repetitions. I was so fucked.

I worked my muscles beyond pain. I didn't even know if I was doing the movements correctly. Something else possessed me, and my body had become Jell-O.

Beau shot me a concerned look. "Feel free to reduce your reps. We all have days where six feels better than ten. And of course, there is no shame in doing the modification. Better to have correct form than to stress out your body."

I was in a whirlwind of exercise. Kettlebell swings turning into squats, burpees combining shoulder lifts. At this point, sweat practically had me shrink-wrapped in my T-shirt.

By the end of the class, I went from gym grunter to gym wailer. I never knew there were levels of annoying sounds one could involuntarily make at the gym. I wasn't doing the last batch of a trillion-billion burpees. My body was doing something else. Sir Hooper had left my body, and her existence was merging with all of life's molecules at the pearly gates of Nirvana.

The lights came on. I did it. I made it through boot camp. I high-fived the beautiful people around me. Not sure if I was still wailing while I did. Now I needed to talk to Beau and tell him I loved him and that I made a mistake, but but but...

First, I needed to go puke.

I burst through the doors of the swanky all-gender bathroom. I ralphed the ralph of a thousand exorcisms. What was supposed to be my grand gesture ended in vomit and using the rim of a toilet seat as an unfortunate headrest.

I heard a gentle rapping at the door. "Sir?"

"Come in." My invitation came out as a groan.

Beau sidled inside and crouched down next to me. "Do you need anything?"

"Probably, like, five Gatorades." Hold on, I wasn't done puking my guts out. "This was supposed to be my grand gesture. Proof I'm not a quitter. That if I want something badly enough, I'll do anything for it."

"It's just a digital badge, Sir. It's no big deal."

"No, I wanted to show you that I love you through..." I gestured across the tiny, tiny expanse of the bathroom cubicle.

"You love me?"

"Of course I do. I was just too chicken shit to admit it." *Retch!* "The last time I loved something this much, I lost it. And I'm going to give separating love from grief a good college try in therapy." *Retch!* "This is a new start for me, and I want you to be a part of it, Beau. That is if you'll have me." *Retch!*

"This might be the most romantic thing someone has ever done for me."

I waved a weak hand holding a puke–blotted tissue. "Get used to it, bub. I want to kiss you, but... I keep barfing." I tucked my arms underneath my chin and considered taking a nap on the bathroom floor.

"I'll kiss you on the forehead."

And he did.

Beau helped scoop me off the floor and assisted me as we moved to the employee break room. I admired EverGreen & Fit's commitment to green. The tables were a mint green whereas the plastic chairs were a deep evergreen. The rest of the break room was accented with pine wood and frosted glass, a chimera of modern design. Sitting down, I chugged a bottle of a sports drink as if my life depended on it.

When I finally had enough electrolytes to stop feeling like a used gym sock, Beau told me how his audition went. At first, he wanted to turn around and head back home. They had auditioned a score of fit men with brown hair and brown eyes. His themed class that we came up with gave him the edge he needed to stand out among a crowd of doppelgängers.

I recounted my struggle to cheat on him with another obnoxious, color-centric gym. "The whole time I was thinking about what you would do and say in the situation. It made me realize how amazing you are." He held my hand across the table and smoothed his thumb over the top of it. I had missed these moments of affection when we were apart. "Does this make you my boyfriend?"

"I'll be your boyfriend if you'll be my girlfriend."

"Deal."

After the trial period, Beau appeared on the app. Occasionally, I would go to his parents' house to watch clips of his workouts. We gathered in the living room to watch someone workout on the television while we sat eating popcorn. His popularity on the app skyrocketed when some clips of his rides went viral on social media. In the clips, he wore a smaller, non-prescription version of his horned-rimmed glasses. He perched them on his nose, claimed he was taking riders to the library, and he would tastefully describe some smut we had read together. People liked Beau's book recommendations. He said producers are toying with releasing his "Dom Next Door" cycling series February next year.

Online, my cartoons spoke to millennials in existential crisis who swarmed to my page to see the next upload. My biggest boost came when Preeti re-shared my cartoon to her wider audience, describing my art as "for those who've struggled with adulthood and grown up reading *Calvin and Hobbes*." My page's visit count increased exponentially, and I was able to monetize and blue check mark that shit. I even made a bit of cash selling merch with a cartoon version of me and Randy, my partner-in-crime baby. It was as if my ItsyBizzy store hadn't been a complete failure.

With my money from selling Chris and Claire my portion of the home, I had a down payment to buy a shop front and an apartment above it in San Francisco. Not the easiest market to get a foothold in, but a startup that dwindled when everyone started to work at home was happy to get an empty property off their hands. My ex-husband was no longer my landlord.

I contacted Perry to see if he'd actually be interested in investing in my business, print shop by day, art studio by night. Moving from the shining 'burbs to the city while inflation was high and the tech bros fled to unregulated states actually saved money. So, he took me up on the offer. We bought equipment off Tina—I made sure to get the paper cutter sharpened. I had a little at-home business and took a lot of customer orders online. For those who threatened to take their business to a store online, I had become both. Shake ye in despair, competitors!

With Beau's hectic schedule, I offered my apartment as a way to reduce his commute, which he took. Of course, we had to re-christen every room with sex.

So Carol and Les didn't feel left out of our lives, we reported for chore duties every other weekend. When Beau showed me the framed cocktail napkin his mother had shared with me earlier, I pretended it was the first time seeing it in a frame.

He mounted it on the wall of our living room when we stopped bullshitting each other, and he moved in.

Epilogue

"**H**oly shit! I think this thing is a safety hazard!" Beau had turned on Georgia the Destroyer of Clits.

I was naked, tied up by my robe tie—this time attached to my bed because we kinksters bought a headboard with posts. I had graduated to the biggest bulb in my collection and was already squirming and aching from the full sensation of it. And the full attention Beau was giving my body with my toys. He was always a firm believer that accessories strengthened our practices.

He lay on his side fully clothed, propping his head up with one hand as the other controlled Georgia. He massaged the outside of my boob with it; the pulse from it pulled my nipple tight and sent a message straight to my aching core. My back arched off the bed as the dual sensations in my pelvis worked together to drive me into a frenzy.

He did the same to my other boob, ever the believer in what someone did with one side, they had to do with the other to maintain proper balance and form. Then he ran Georgia under my belly button. Vibrations bounced between the bigger plug and my clit. He wasn't hitting the spot and yet, hit the spot from multiple directions. I squirmed and kicked; my wrists held lightly in place by the tie of my robe.

He kneeled, sitting on one of my legs and gripping the other firmly at my thigh. It was to keep me from thrashing. He guided the thing along the inside of my leg. The toy buzzing at the crease of my thigh wound me so tightly. I throbbed with a needy little pain. Beau forcing me to be still compounded the pleasure.

Georgia grazed just to the right of my clit and the left. I had lost any control over my moans. They were cries wrung out from his playfulness. Finally, he sicced Georgia on my swollen bud. I came in an instant. It was like being at the end of his advanced boot camp all over again.

"You like being full," he taunted as he let go of my thigh and slicked his thumb with my pleasure. He held my face, shoving his soaked thumb into my mouth. "You love feeling me in every one of your needy little holes."

I sucked his thumb and hummed with how delicious he'd get me to taste. I nodded desperately.

He rolled off me and stood up, gently guiding me on to my stomach. He propped my belly with a pillow to raise my ass higher in the air. His clothes hit my floor, and I heard the pump of lube.

"Look at me," he ordered.

I rested my cheek on the mattress and turned my gaze toward him. My sunshine man had surrendered to his dark, ravenous side. He glowered as he stroked himself with his lubed hand, his cock dusky and hard.

His other hand tugged the bulb free from my ass. He tossed it somewhere on the bed where it landed with a muted *thud*. As the hand that pleasured himself rotated from the middle part of his shaft to over his tip, his other hand massaged my aperture. It was so hot looking at him possessed with desire. I attempted to hump the pillow beneath my belly to take care of my aching need.

A hard smack landed on my ass, which sent my eyes rolling in the back of my head. "Beg for it."

"Fuck me," I moaned.

Another smack on my other cheek. "Where do you want me?" His fingers circled exactly where.

"My ass, Coach."

He pumped more lube. His weight behind me on the mattress shifted. The crown of his bare cock pressed against me. He nudged in, made it past the first tight ring. He rubbed my hip as I adjusted to the invasion, a different sensation from the plugs or his fingers. The discomfort became a new boundary crossed, and I took more of him inside me. I shivered; a cold sweat tingled over my skin. He caressed my back, telling me what a good girl I was, and I pushed myself all the way into him, feeling his hips meet my ass.

I trembled, much like my first time but so much better, because he loved me, and I loved him. And his careful attention and adoration fortified the trust between us. I couldn't wait for more future with him, more adventures.

His deft fingers targeted my sweet spot as he gently moved inside me.

"Are you good?" he asked.

"So, so, good." My husky voice overran with desire. "Your good girl." I widened my knees and felt him go deeper as I stretched around him.

My eager and relaxed body invited him for more. He pulled all the way out of me so I wiggled my hips to plead for that feeling again. Then he entered me, powerful and swift. My breath ripped from my throat.

"I'm going to come embarrassingly soon," he whispered weakly against my temple, as if the pumps I was giving him were draining him of his life force. His breathing quickened. "Oh Sir." He left me with a pop, the heat of his cum laced my lower back. He squeezed my cheeks around his cock as he continued to pump and coat me in every last drop of him.

He flopped next to me and untied my hands. I crossed them underneath my chin as I let the new sensations wash over me. The gentle bristle of a hand towel cleaned some of him off me.

"How was that?" His voice was still breathless.

"Not something I'd want to do every day but—" I chuckled. It was one of the hottest things I'd ever done in a top ten list of hot acts. And Beau's name was by every single one like a series of high scores at an arcade.

I wasn't sure if any words could quite capture what it felt to have a lover so committed to exploring new things with me. It made me feel the sexiest I ever felt, but it also was comforting—that I somehow wasn't a deviant with some unexplored trauma. I was just me sharing my body with him because I loved him. "Maybe we save it for special occasions—holidays, birthdays," I said.

"Special occasion, hmm?"

I nodded, my eyes closed, still rolling in the fugue. The weight shifted in the bed as Beau reached for something. It sounded as if he fidgeted in the pockets of his pants. He returned to bed.

"How about we make tonight extra special, then?" He brushed a hand against my cheek. I finally opened my eyes.

Right in my face was a square-cut ruby and gold ring. "The fuck?!" I popped up in bed.

"Saoirse Hooper, will you—"

"You can't propose to me with your dick out." I sprung out of bed and scrambled for my satin nightie crinkled on the floor. He stepped into his boxers and walked on his knees to me.

"Saoirse will—"

"Yes!"

"I haven't even asked yet."

"Sorry. Nervous."

"I have no idea what the future will hold, but the one sure thing I want is you by my side. Will you marry me, Saoirse Hooper?"

Tears spilled from my eyes. All I could do was nod.

Maybe my printing business will flop. Maybe it will succeed. Maybe Beau will take the fitness world by storm. Maybe he won't. But who am I kidding? He definitely will. Maybe the only baby I'll have is a cartoon one who has conversations with me about the emotions I find hard to process. Maybe Beau and I will have our rainbow baby. Or maybe our rainbow child is waiting for us to find them.

What is a constant in my visions of the future is Beau because he wants the best for me, even if I'm the one standing in my own way.

Whatever we do, I will give it my all. No foot pointed in the direction of the exit. I *will* ride that beak in a metaphorical sense. Up until this year, I had never won anything in my life, but I think it was because life was saving up for me and finally paid me in dividends. Beau helped me uncover a better version of me: fearless and open-minded.

And occasionally, when I'm really excited, I will *woo*.

Acknowledgements

First and foremost, thank you readers. Without you, I couldn't continue this author journey. If you've read my darkish superhero romance *and* my goofy rom com *and* want to continue to read my forays into romance subgenres, I salute you much like I would the Olympian-like athletes who choose to take advanced workout classes. Spreading the word about my book is also greatly appreciated.

Thank you also to my beta readers, Meredith and Donna. Your feedback helped me refine Sir and this story. I also appreciate the support of my fellow indie authors. If there is a scene you especially like, it probably happened with another indie author playing the devil on my shoulder.

Thank you also to Mel for helping me proofread the proofread so that this book was proofread AF.

Applause and commissions should go to Kate Maxwell, artist extraordinaire, for making Sir's millennial circling the drain cartoons come to life. Enjoy her hard work in *BoJack Horseman, Tuca & Bertie, Velma, Ten Year Old Tom*, and *Final Space*.

You can get most of Sir's T-shirts at my store hosted by Threadless.

And I have unending gratitude to my husband. He is supportive of my dreams, and he knows that, although the workout instructor on the screen elicits a giggle from me, my love is only for him.

Thank you to the fitness app that was especially popular in 2020. The variety of music and instructors, to me, shows that everyone can belong to a gym, and exercise can be enjoyed by every kind of body. And a special thanks to my muse whose classes and double entendres conjured a whole book out of me.

This book was my first NaNoWriMo challenge. I didn't think I could do it with my schedule and demands. Yet when I reached the end, my husband asked me, "What do you win?" A book, Mr. Elise, a book. And a stronger belief in myself.

About the author

Jonesy Elise writes romance inspired by the Saturday morning shows she watched growing up. Her stories are real genre mashers. If she isn't writing those, she's composing contemporary stories about the eccentric people who read her paranormal/sci-fi/romance mashups.

No matter what she writes, the FMC will come to voice, the characters will be memorable, and they'll get their HEA (or HFN).

She likes her romance spicy. So, read with a glass of milk.

She is an Iowa transplant living in the Bay Area with her family and dog. She loves karaoking to Alanis Morrisette, completing yoga with all the props, and attending rock concerts with cool people. She is an unabashed caffeine addict and orders her sugar-free vanilla latte with an extra shot of espresso and a sprinkle of cinnamon. If she isn't sharing the same HILARIOUS raccoon and possum memes repeatedly, you'll find her making goofy videos to promote her books or share about her author life. *Personal Best* is her second book. Keep up with Jonesy and her upcoming projects by visiting her website and signing up for her newsletter at Jonesy Elise Writes Wrongs. Or, feel free to follow her on Instagram @jonesy_elise_writes_wrongs

If you enjoyed this book, she encourages you to review it and shout your love from any kind of rooftop. Spreading the word will help an indie author out.

Other Works

by Jonesy Elise

Saint of the Shadows, a superhero romance series

- *Saint of the Shadows*

  - Also available on paperback.

- *Deus Ex Umbra* expected spring 2025

Short stories

- "Honeymoon of the Lizard Princess"

  - In *Secrets We Keep* anthology October 2024

Contemporary Romance

- *Personal Best*

- *Smalltown Showgirl* expected summer 2025

Printed in Great Britain
by Amazon

48740971R00172